STAR WARS

ADVENTURES

PRINCESS LEIA AND
THE ROYAL RANSOM

visit us at www.abdopublishing.com

Reinforced library bound edition published in 2012 by Spotlight, a division of the
ABDO Group, 8000 West 78th Street, Edina, Minnesota 55439.
Spotlight produces high-quality reinforced library bound editions for schools and
libraries. Published by agreement with Dark Horse Comics, Inc., and Lucasfilm Ltd.
Printed in the United States of America, Melrose Park, Illinois.
052010
092010
This book contains at least 10% recycled materials.

Special thanks to Elaine Mederer, Jann Moorhead, David Anderman,
Leland Chee, Sue Rostoni, and Carol Roeder at Lucas Licensing

Cataloging-in-Publication Data

Barlow, Jeremy.
Star wars adventures: Princess Leia and the royal ransom /
   script Jeremy Barlow ; art Carlo Soriano ; colors Michael Atiyeh ;
   lettering Michael Heisler ; cover art Sean McNally. -- Reinforced library bound ed.
   p. cm. -- (Star Wars Adventures)
1. Leia, Princess (Fictitious character)--Comic books, strips, etc. 2. Star Wars fiction.
3. Solo, Han (Fictitious character)--Comic books, strips, etc. 4. Graphic novels.
5. Cartoons and comics. 6. Science fiction comic books, strips, etc.
I. Soriano, Carlo. II. Atiyeh, Michael. III. Title.
Summary: Princess Leia, Han Solo, and Chewie are racing to deliver vital information to the Rebel
Alliance. Han allows himself to be distracted with the idea of earning some fast credits.
[741.5'973]--dc22

ISBN 978-1-59961-902-6 (reinforced library bound edition)

All Spotlight books are reinforced library bindings
and manufactured in the United States of America.

STAR WARS ADVENTURES

PRINCESS LEIA AND THE ROYAL RANSOM

Script **Jeremy Barlow**

Art **Carlo Soriano**

Colors **Michael Atiyeh**

Lettering **Michael Heisler**

Cover art **Sean McNally**

Dark Horse Books®

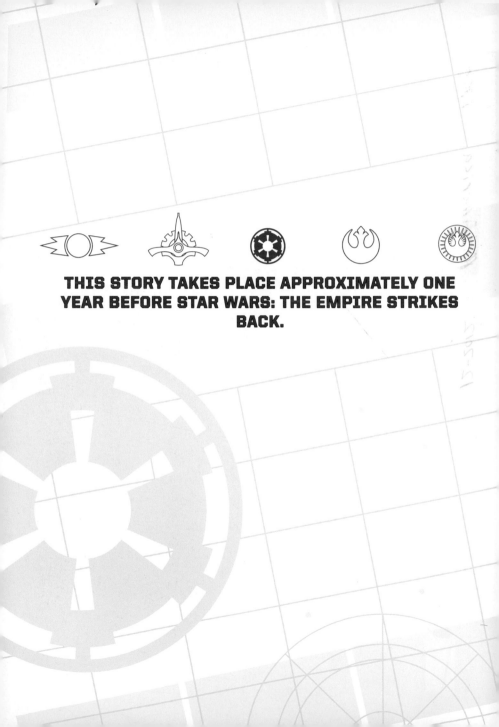

THIS STORY TAKES PLACE APPROXIMATELY ONE YEAR BEFORE STAR WARS: THE EMPIRE STRIKES BACK.

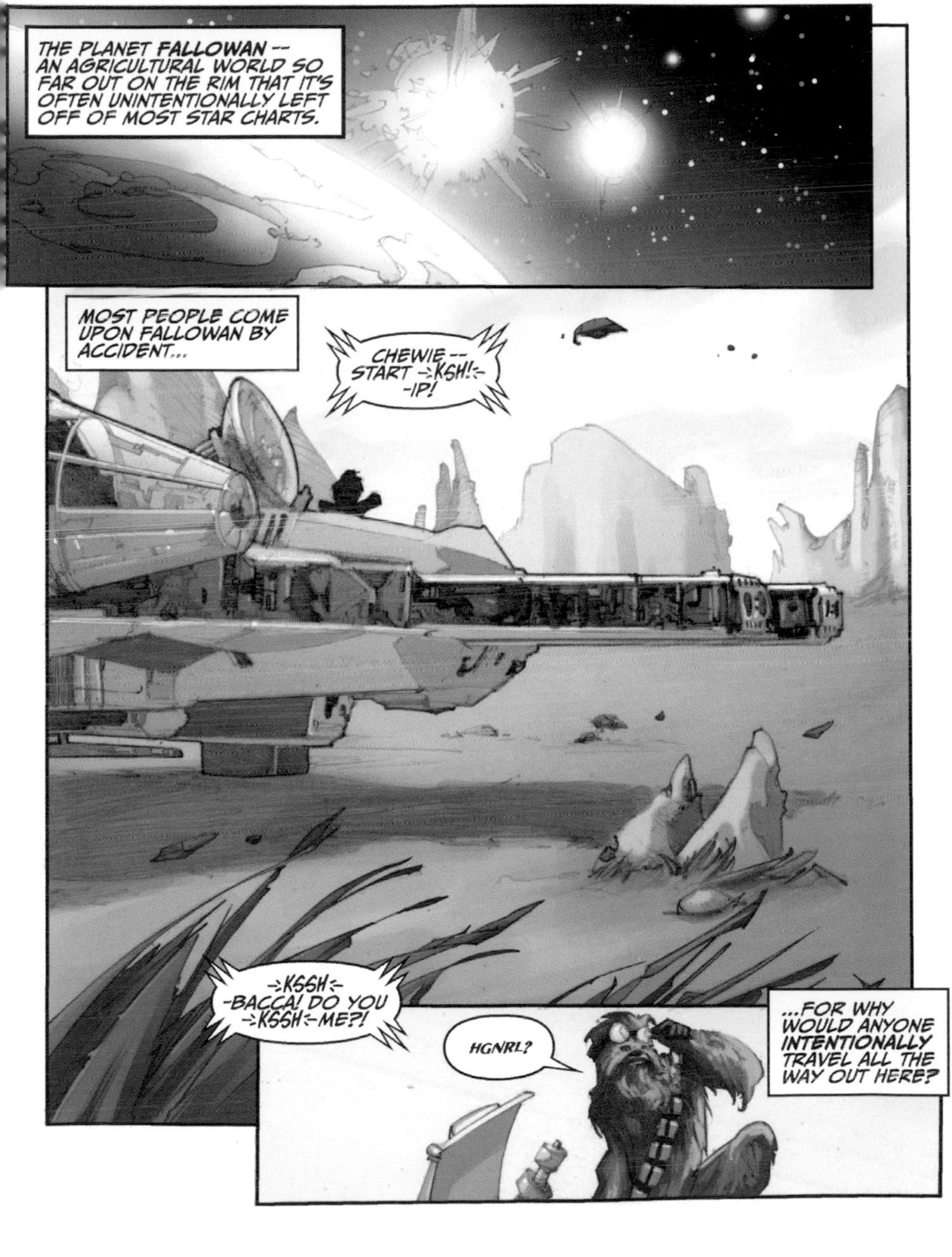
THE PLANET FALLOWAN -- AN AGRICULTURAL WORLD SO FAR OUT ON THE RIM THAT IT'S OFTEN UNINTENTIONALLY LEFT OFF OF MOST STAR CHARTS.
MOST PEOPLE COME UPON FALLOWAN BY ACCIDENT...
CHEWIE -- START -KSH!- -IP!
-KSSH- -BACCA! DO YOU -KSSH- ME?!
HGNRL?
...FOR WHY WOULD ANYONE INTENTIONALLY TRAVEL ALL THE WAY OUT HERE?

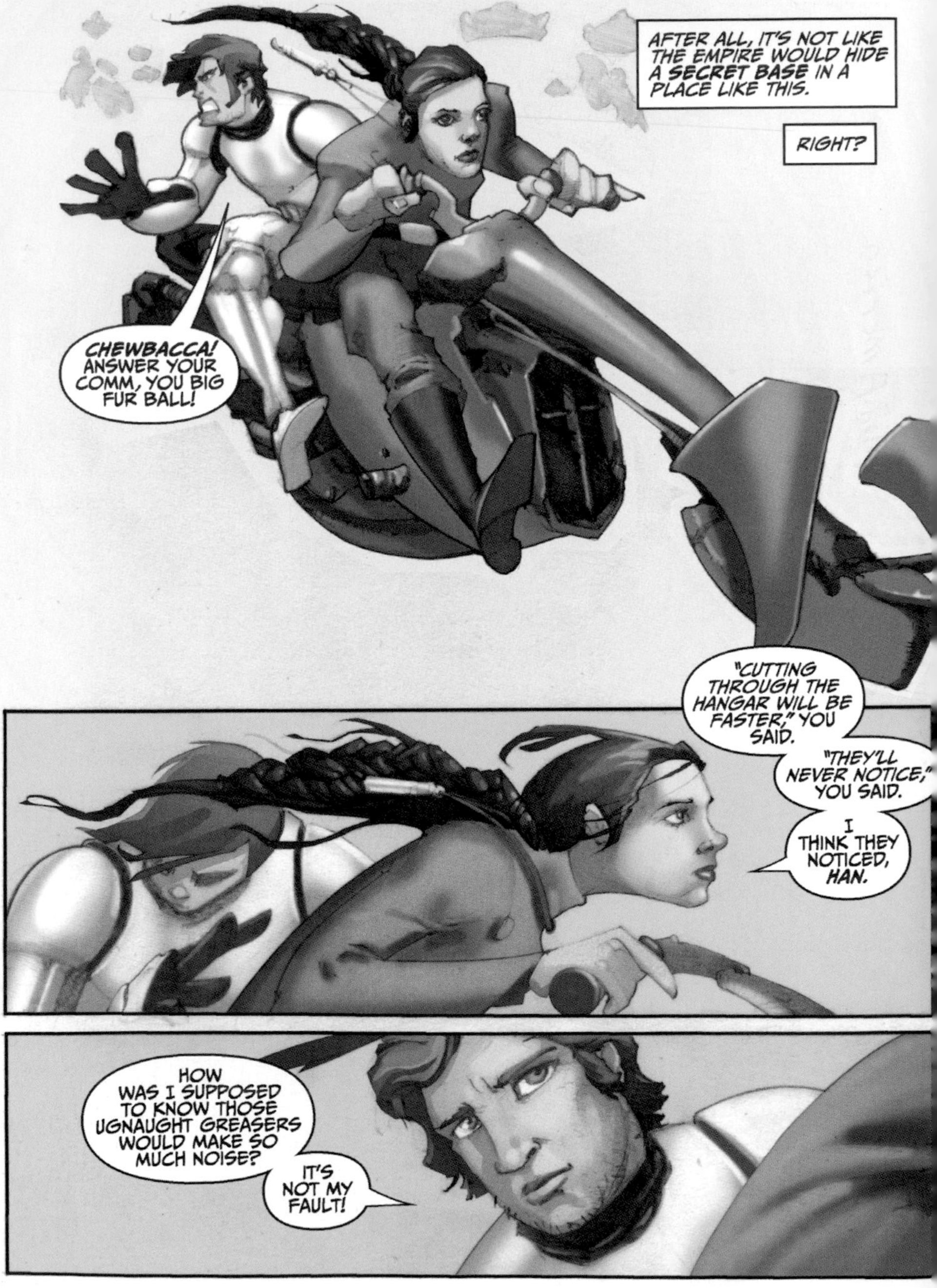
AFTER ALL, IT'S NOT LIKE THE EMPIRE WOULD HIDE A **SECRET BASE** IN A PLACE LIKE THIS.
RIGHT?
CHEWBACCA! ANSWER YOUR COMM, YOU BIG FUR BALL!
"CUTTING THROUGH THE HANGAR WILL BE FASTER," YOU SAID.
"THEY'LL NEVER NOTICE," YOU SAID.
I THINK THEY NOTICED, **HAN.**
HOW WAS I SUPPOSED TO KNOW THOSE UGNAUGHT GREASERS WOULD MAKE SO MUCH NOISE?
IT'S NOT MY FAULT!

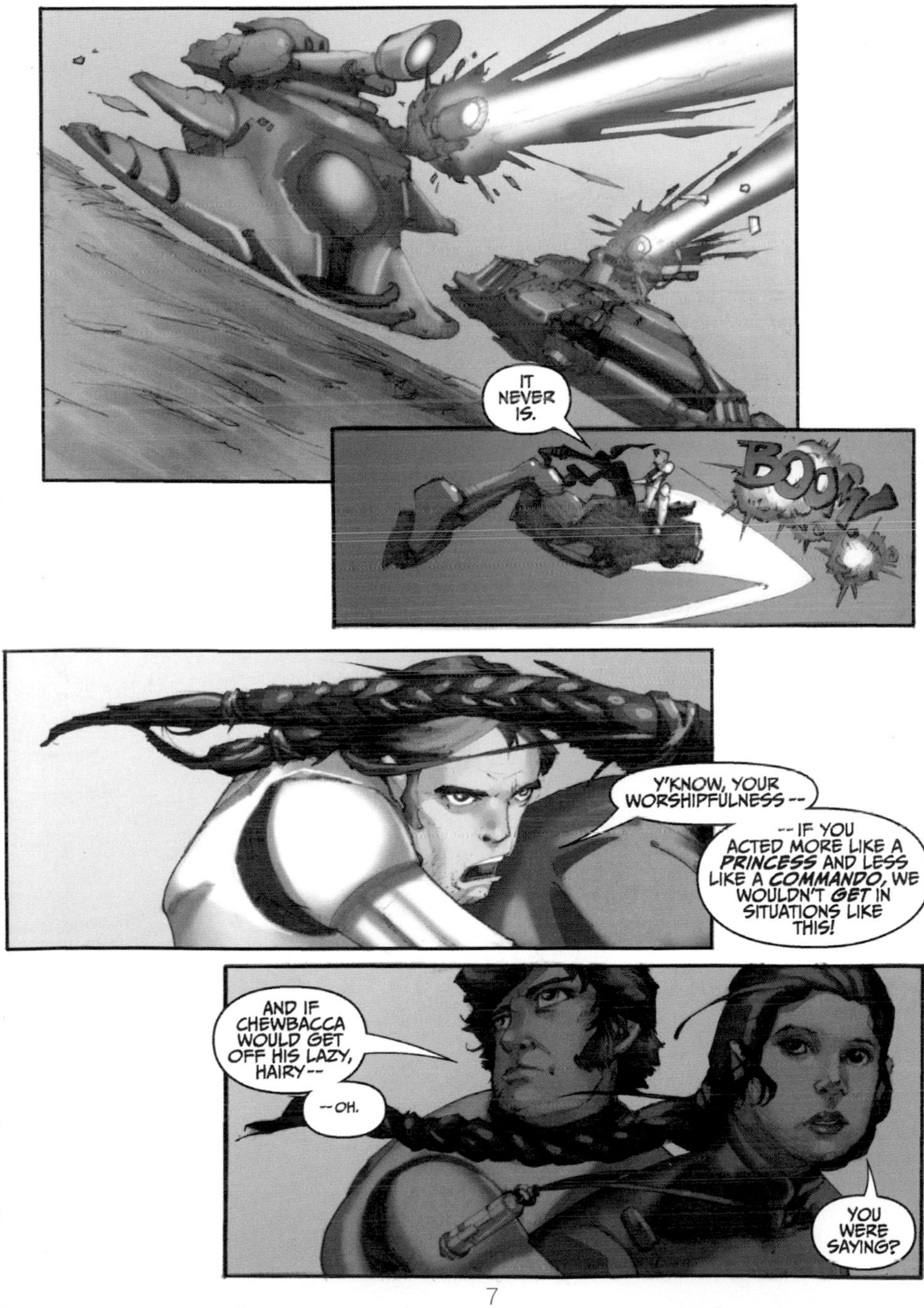
IT NEVER IS.
BOOM!
Y'KNOW, YOUR WORSHIPFULNESS --
-- IF YOU ACTED MORE LIKE A **PRINCESS** AND LESS LIKE A **COMMANDO**, WE WOULDN'T **GET** IN SITUATIONS LIKE THIS!
AND IF CHEWBACCA WOULD GET OFF HIS LAZY, HAIRY--
--OH.
YOU WERE SAYING?

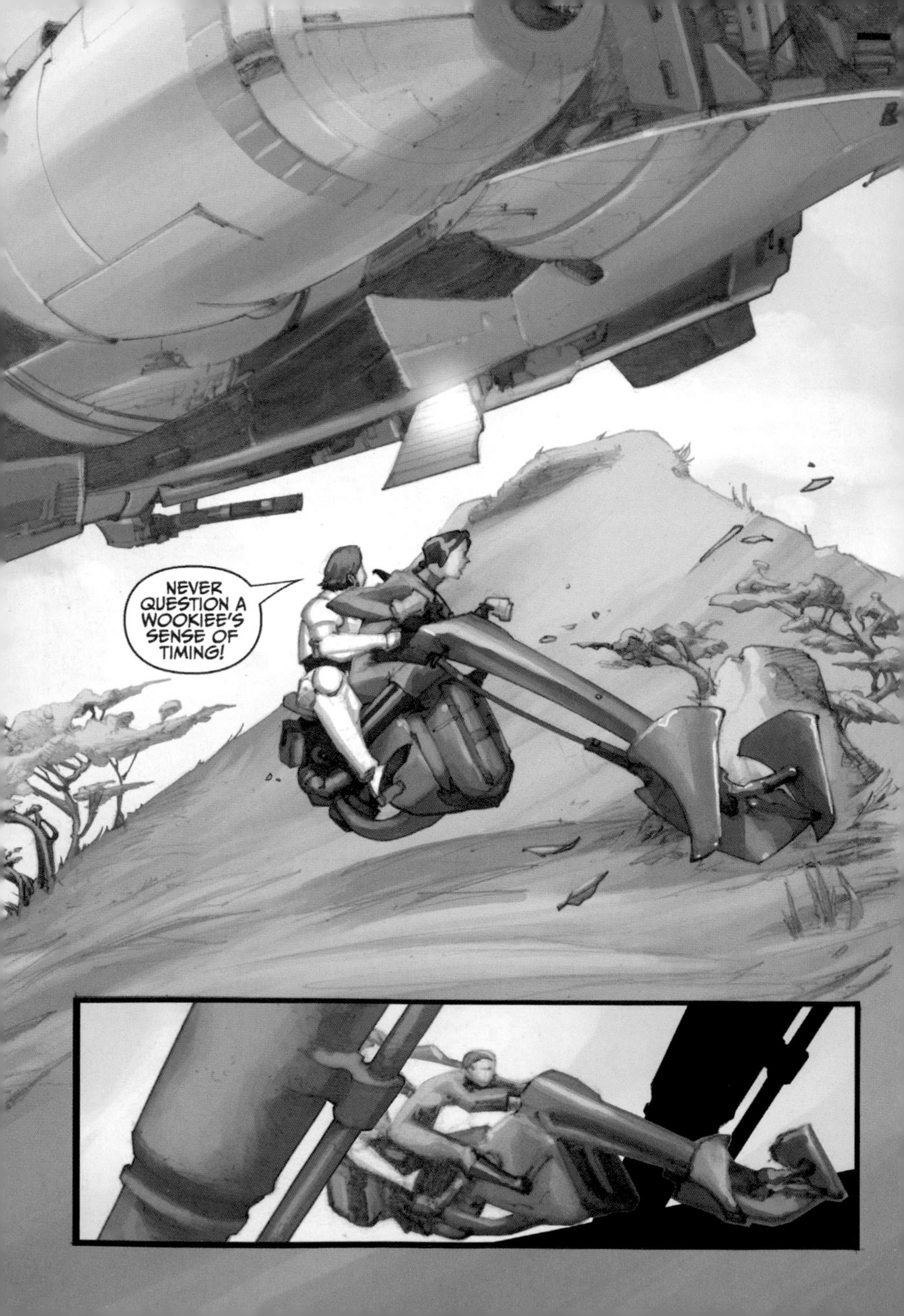
NEVER QUESTION A WOOKIEE'S SENSE OF TIMING!

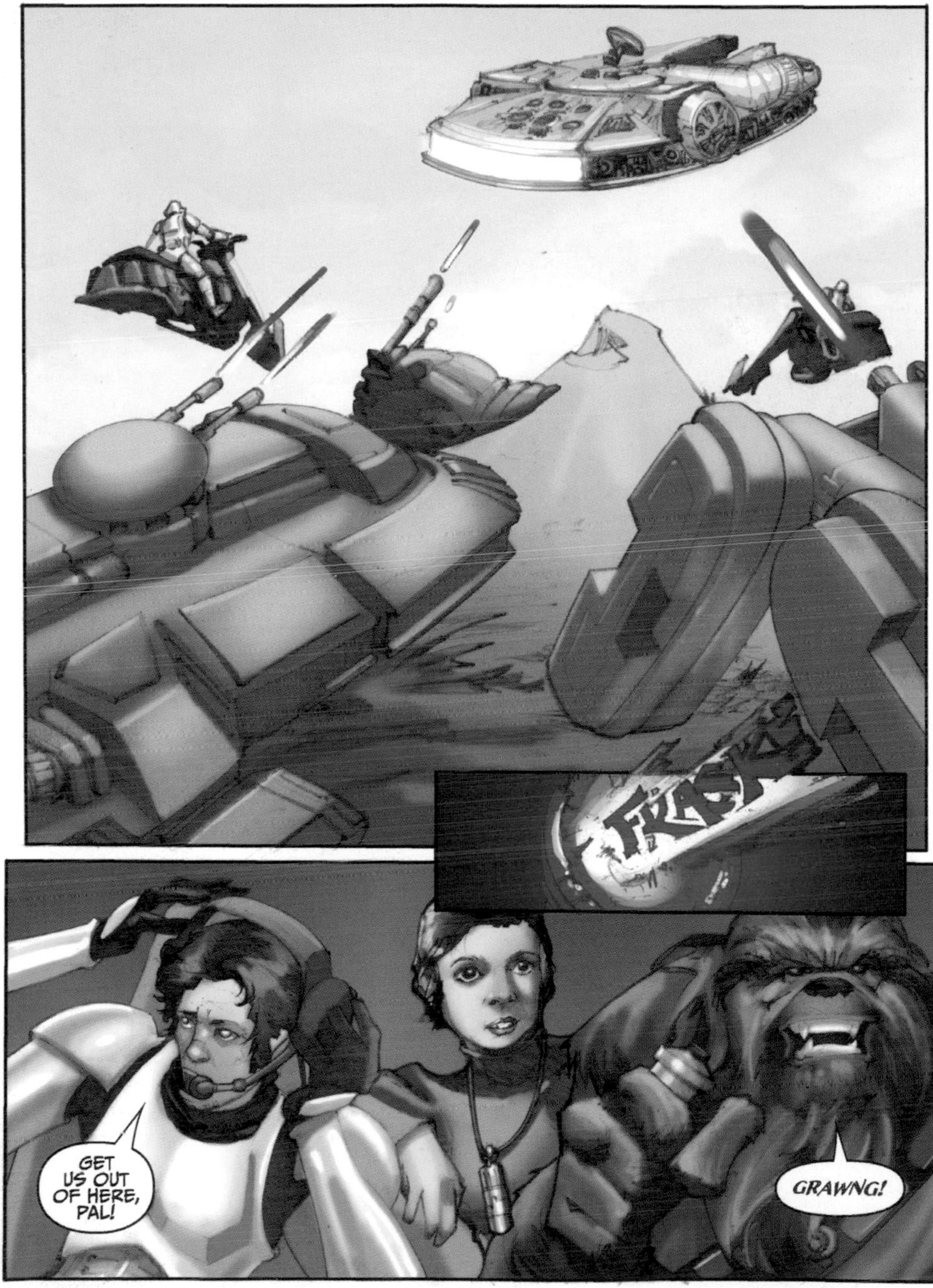
FRASK!
GET US OUT OF HERE, PAL!
GRAWNG!

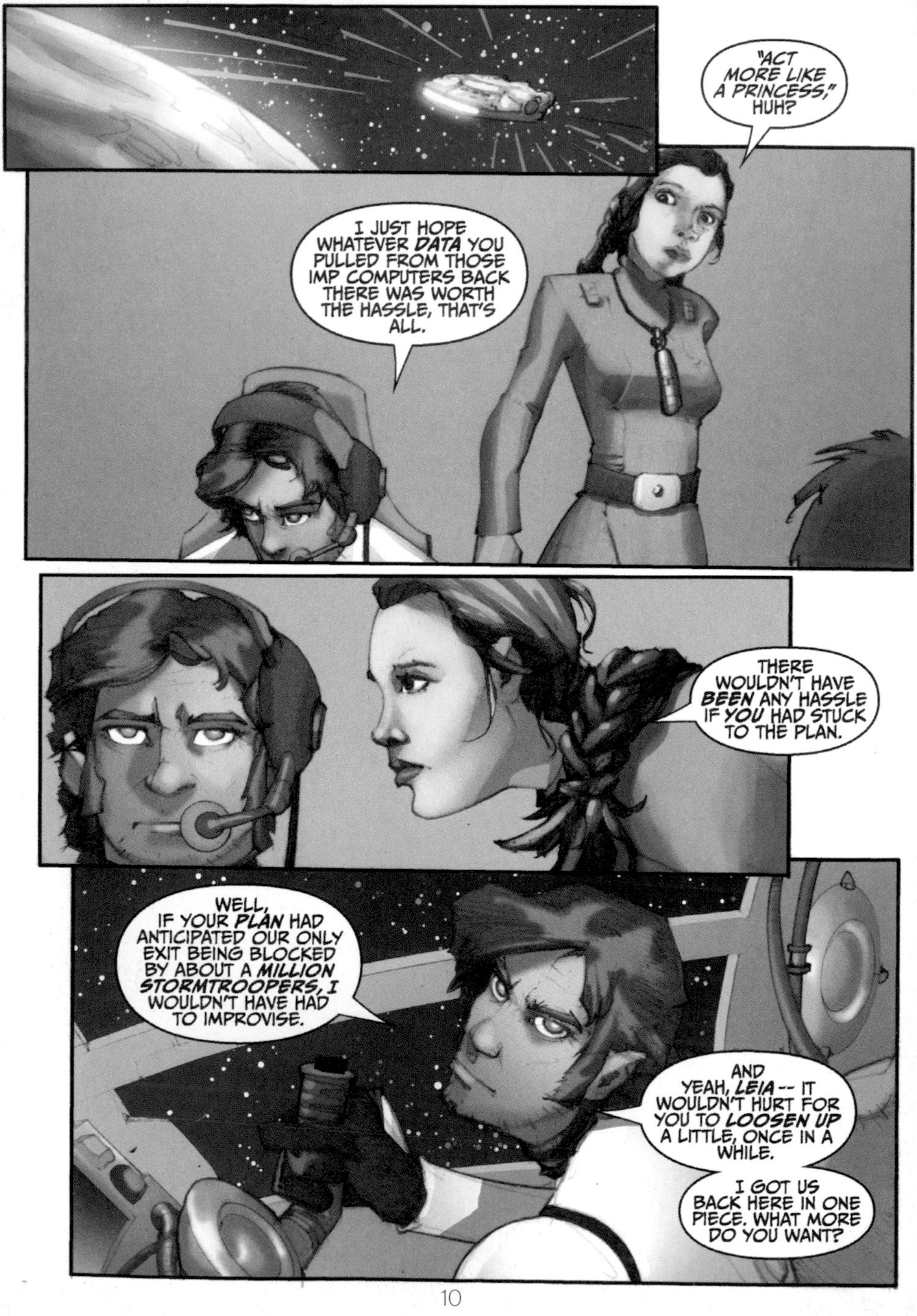
"ACT MORE LIKE A PRINCESS," HUH?
I JUST HOPE WHATEVER DATA YOU PULLED FROM THOSE IMP COMPUTERS BACK THERE WAS WORTH THE HASSLE, THAT'S ALL.
THERE WOULDN'T HAVE BEEN ANY HASSLE IF YOU HAD STUCK TO THE PLAN.
WELL, IF YOUR PLAN HAD ANTICIPATED OUR ONLY EXIT BEING BLOCKED BY ABOUT A MILLION STORMTROOPERS, I WOULDN'T HAVE HAD TO IMPROVISE.
AND YEAH, LEIA -- IT WOULDN'T HURT FOR YOU TO LOOSEN UP A LITTLE, ONCE IN A WHILE.
I GOT US BACK HERE IN ONE PIECE. WHAT MORE DO YOU WANT?

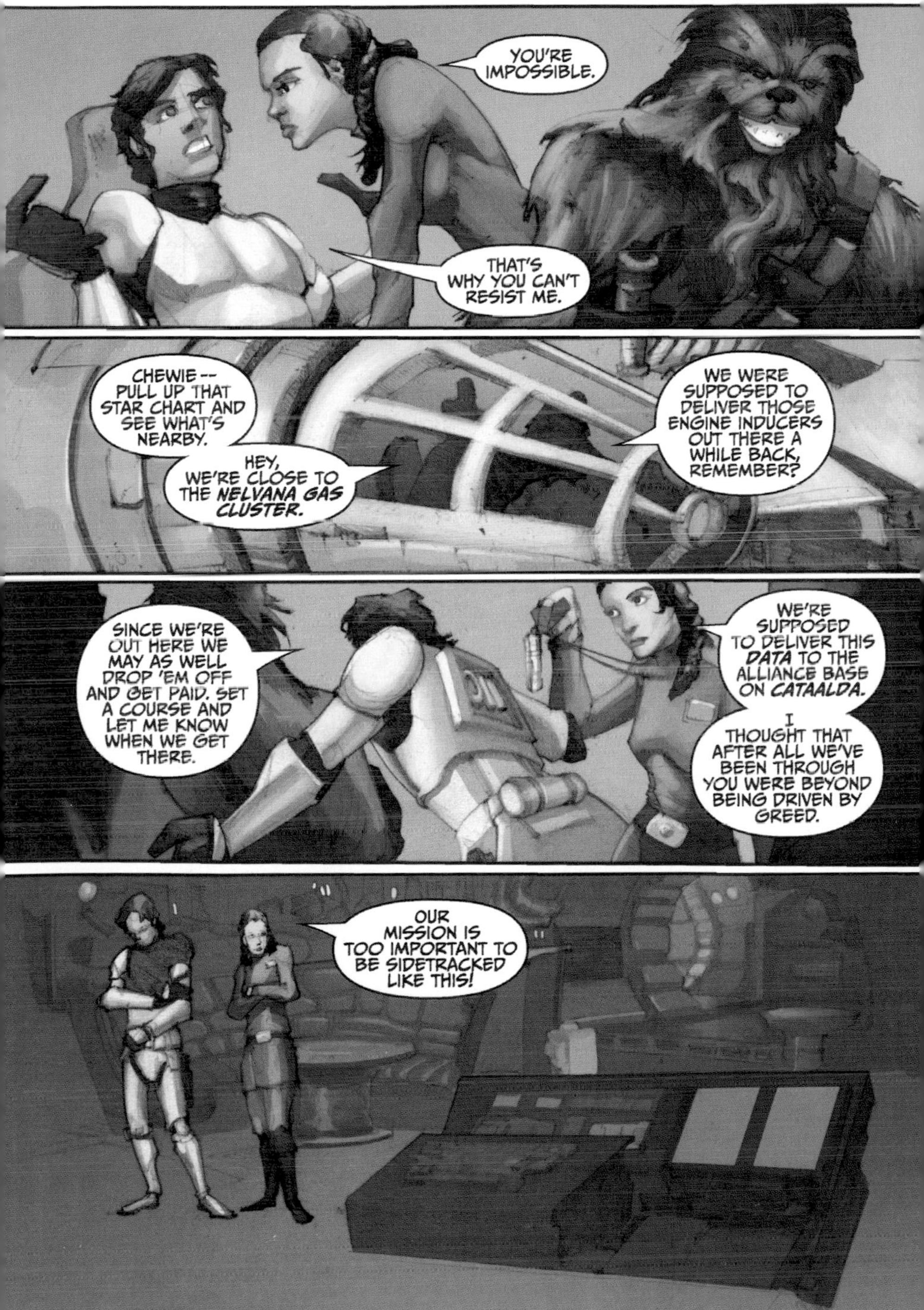
YOU'RE IMPOSSIBLE.
THAT'S WHY YOU CAN'T RESIST ME.
CHEWIE -- PULL UP THAT STAR CHART AND SEE WHAT'S NEARBY.
HEY, WE'RE CLOSE TO THE *NELVANA GAS CLUSTER.*
WE WERE SUPPOSED TO DELIVER THOSE ENGINE INDUCERS OUT THERE A WHILE BACK, REMEMBER?
SINCE WE'RE OUT HERE WE MAY AS WELL DROP 'EM OFF AND GET PAID. SET A COURSE AND LET ME KNOW WHEN WE GET THERE.
WE'RE SUPPOSED TO DELIVER THIS *DATA* TO THE ALLIANCE BASE ON *CATAALDA.*
I THOUGHT THAT AFTER ALL WE'VE BEEN THROUGH YOU WERE BEYOND BEING DRIVEN BY GREED.
OUR MISSION IS TOO IMPORTANT TO BE SIDETRACKED LIKE THIS!

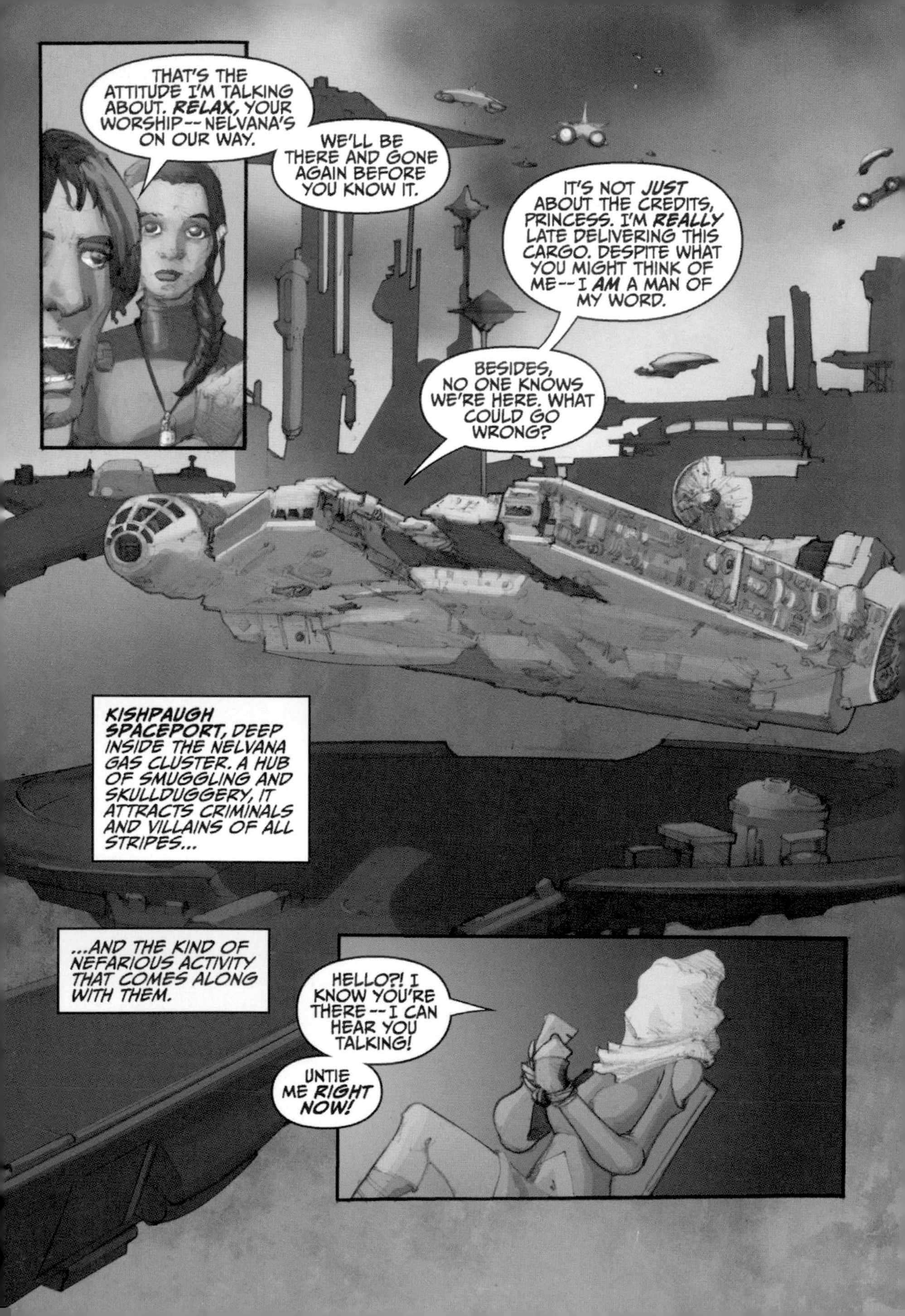
THAT'S THE ATTITUDE I'M TALKING ABOUT. **RELAX,** YOUR WORSHIP-- NELVANA'S ON OUR WAY.
WE'LL BE THERE AND GONE AGAIN BEFORE YOU KNOW IT.
IT'S NOT **JUST** ABOUT THE CREDITS, PRINCESS. I'M **REALLY** LATE DELIVERING THIS CARGO. DESPITE WHAT YOU MIGHT THINK OF ME-- I **AM** A MAN OF MY WORD.
BESIDES, NO ONE KNOWS WE'RE HERE. WHAT COULD GO WRONG?
KISHPAUGH SPACEPORT, DEEP INSIDE THE NELVANA GAS CLUSTER. A HUB OF SMUGGLING AND SKULLDUGGERY, IT ATTRACTS CRIMINALS AND VILLAINS OF ALL STRIPES...
...AND THE KIND OF NEFARIOUS ACTIVITY THAT COMES ALONG WITH THEM.
HELLO?! I KNOW YOU'RE THERE-- I CAN HEAR YOU TALKING!
UNTIE ME **RIGHT NOW!**

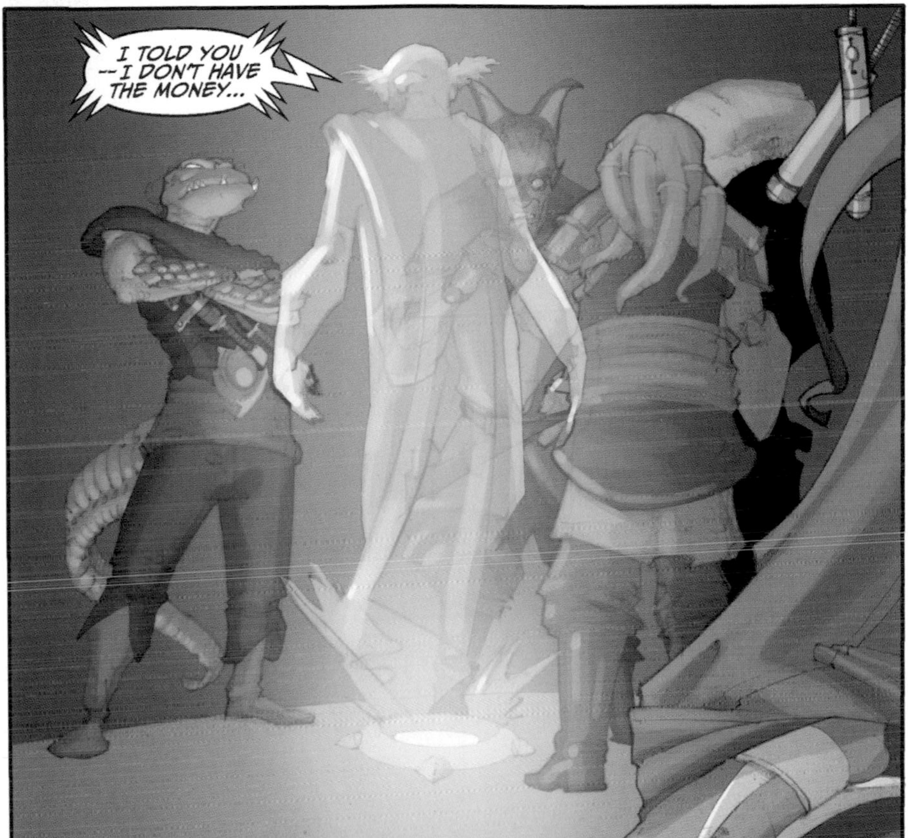
I TOLD YOU --I DON'T HAVE THE MONEY...

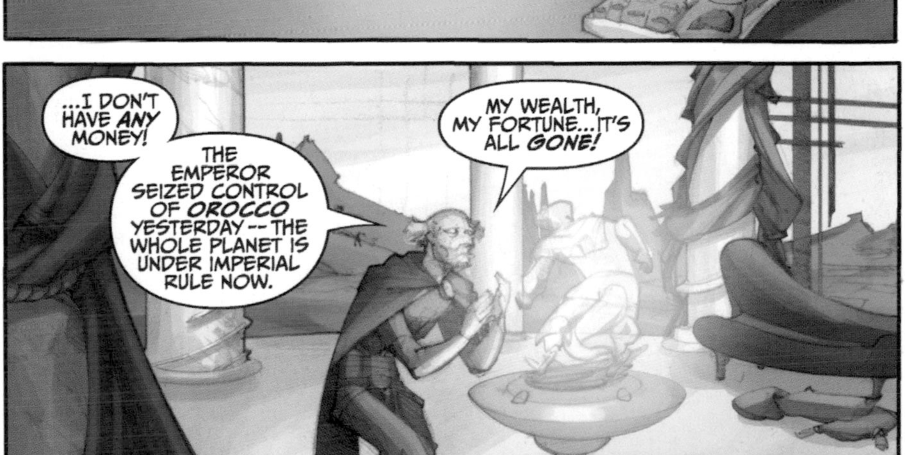
...I DON'T HAVE ANY MONEY!
THE EMPEROR SEIZED CONTROL OF OROCCO YESTERDAY--THE WHOLE PLANET IS UNDER IMPERIAL RULE NOW.
MY WEALTH, MY FORTUNE...IT'S ALL GONE!

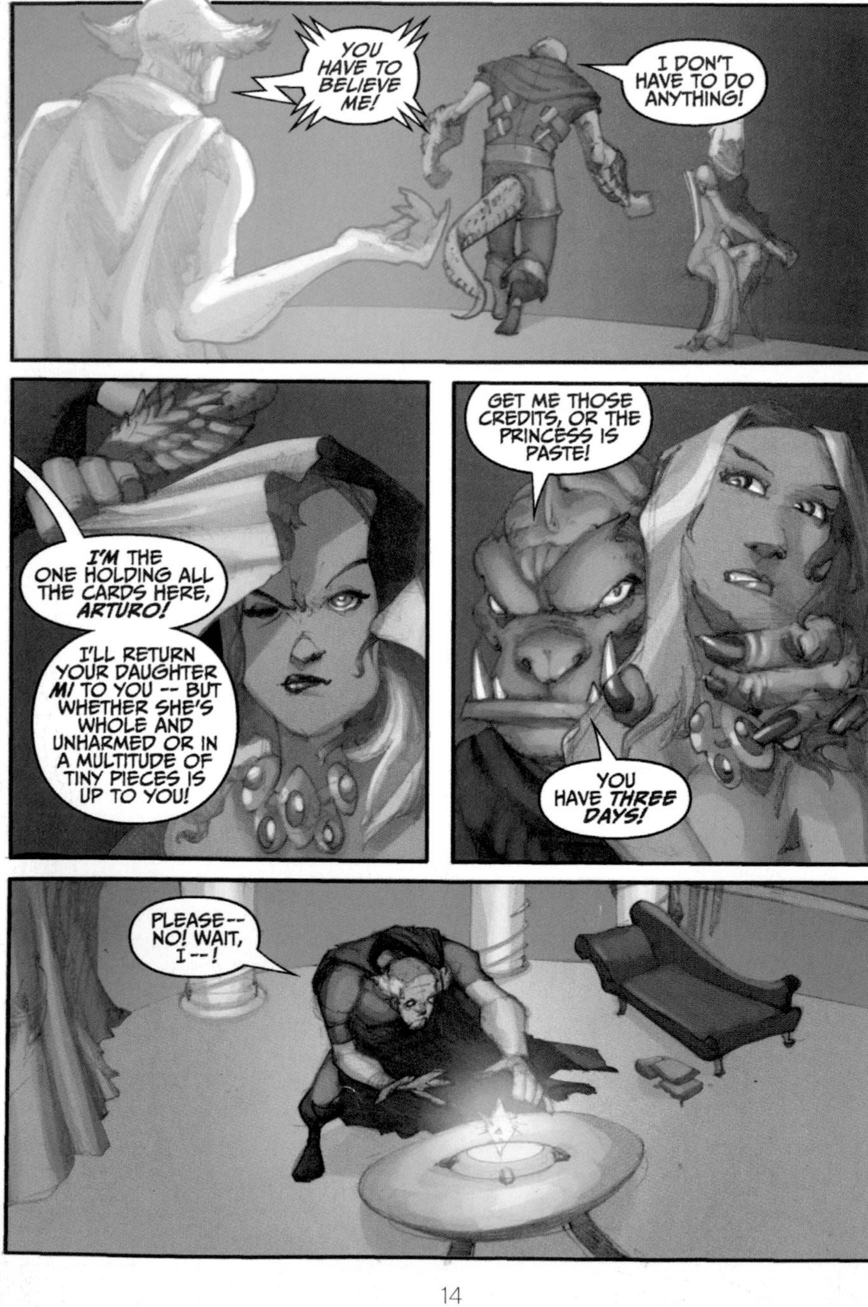
YOU HAVE TO BELIEVE ME!
I DON'T HAVE TO DO ANYTHING!
I'M THE ONE HOLDING ALL THE CARDS HERE, ARTURO!
I'LL RETURN YOUR DAUGHTER MI TO YOU -- BUT WHETHER SHE'S WHOLE AND UNHARMED OR IN A MULTITUDE OF TINY PIECES IS UP TO YOU!
GET ME THOSE CREDITS, OR THE PRINCESS IS PASTE!
YOU HAVE THREE DAYS!
PLEASE-- NO! WAIT, I--!

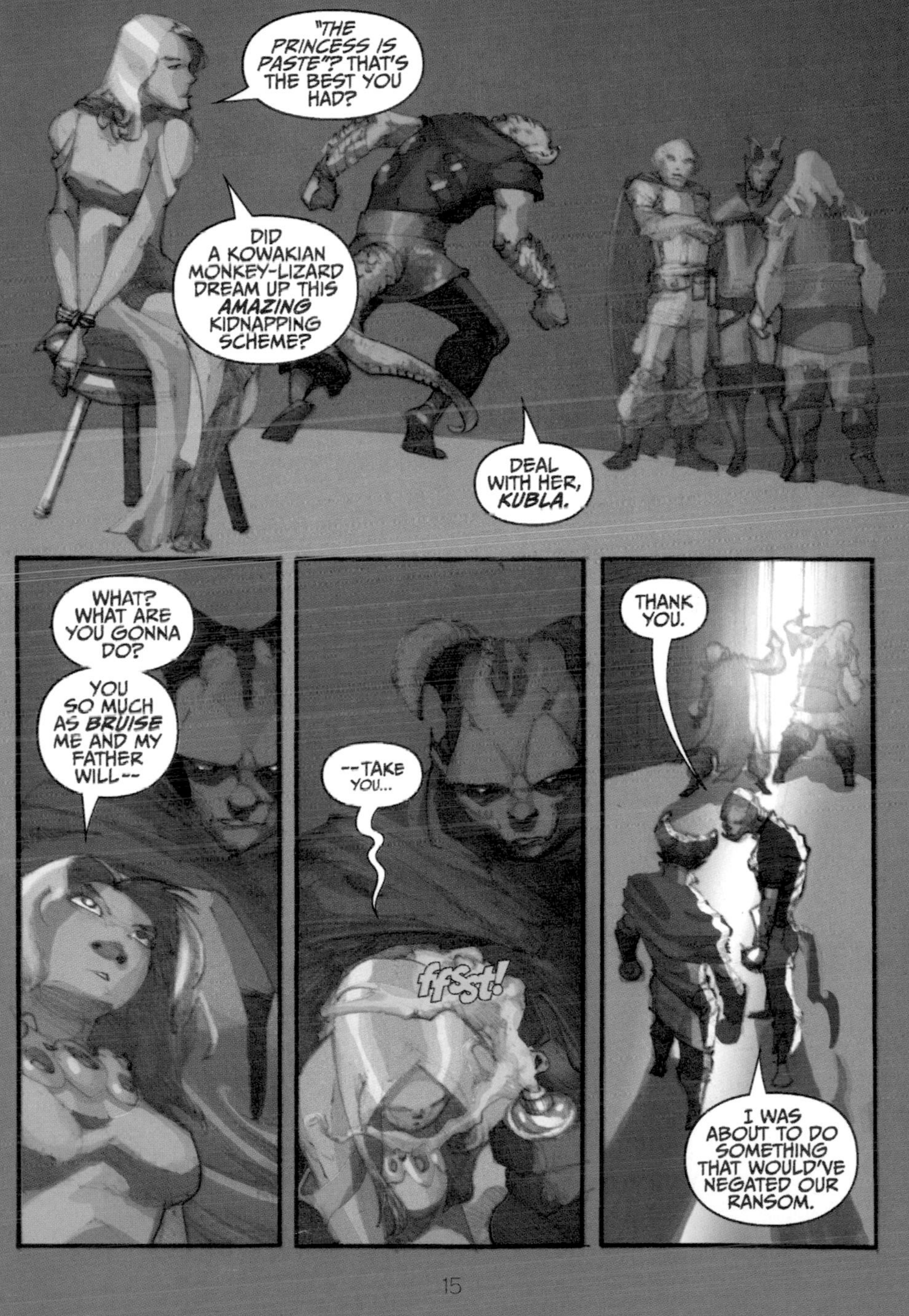
"THE PRINCESS IS PASTE"? THAT'S THE BEST YOU HAD?
DID A KOWAKIAN MONKEY-LIZARD DREAM UP THIS *AMAZING* KIDNAPPING SCHEME?
DEAL WITH HER, *KUBLA.*
WHAT? WHAT ARE YOU GONNA DO?
YOU SO MUCH AS *BRUISE* ME AND MY FATHER WILL--
--TAKE YOU...
ffst!
THANK YOU.
I WAS ABOUT TO DO SOMETHING THAT WOULD'VE NEGATED OUR RANSOM.

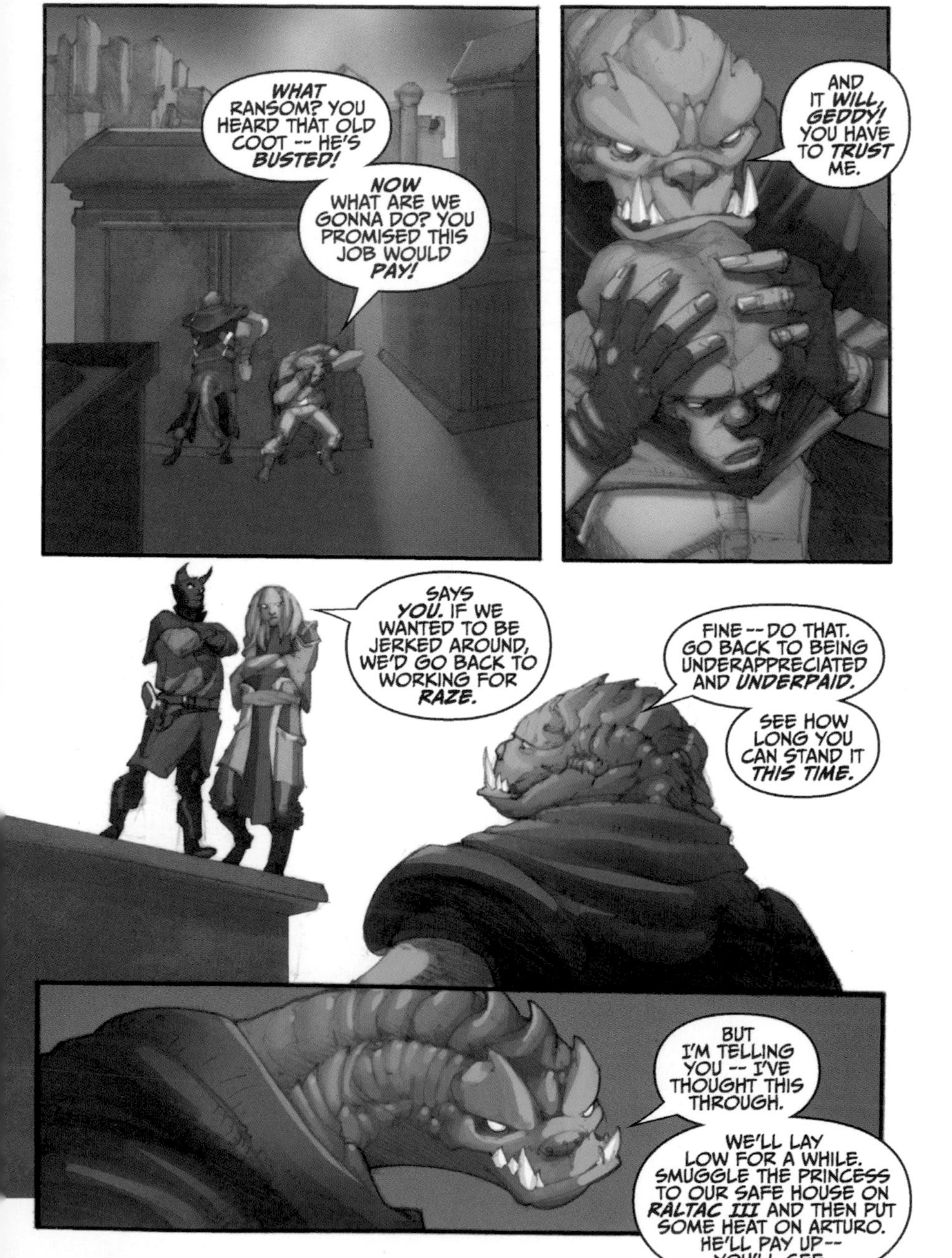
WHAT RANSOM? YOU HEARD THAT OLD COOT -- HE'S BUSTED!
NOW WHAT ARE WE GONNA DO? YOU PROMISED THIS JOB WOULD PAY!
AND IT WILL, GEDDY! YOU HAVE TO TRUST ME.
SAYS YOU. IF WE WANTED TO BE JERKED AROUND, WE'D GO BACK TO WORKING FOR RAZE.
FINE -- DO THAT. GO BACK TO BEING UNDERAPPRECIATED AND UNDERPAID.
SEE HOW LONG YOU CAN STAND IT THIS TIME.
BUT I'M TELLING YOU -- I'VE THOUGHT THIS THROUGH.
WE'LL LAY LOW FOR A WHILE. SMUGGLE THE PRINCESS TO OUR SAFE HOUSE ON RALTAC III AND THEN PUT SOME HEAT ON ARTURO. HE'LL PAY UP-- YOU'LL SEE.

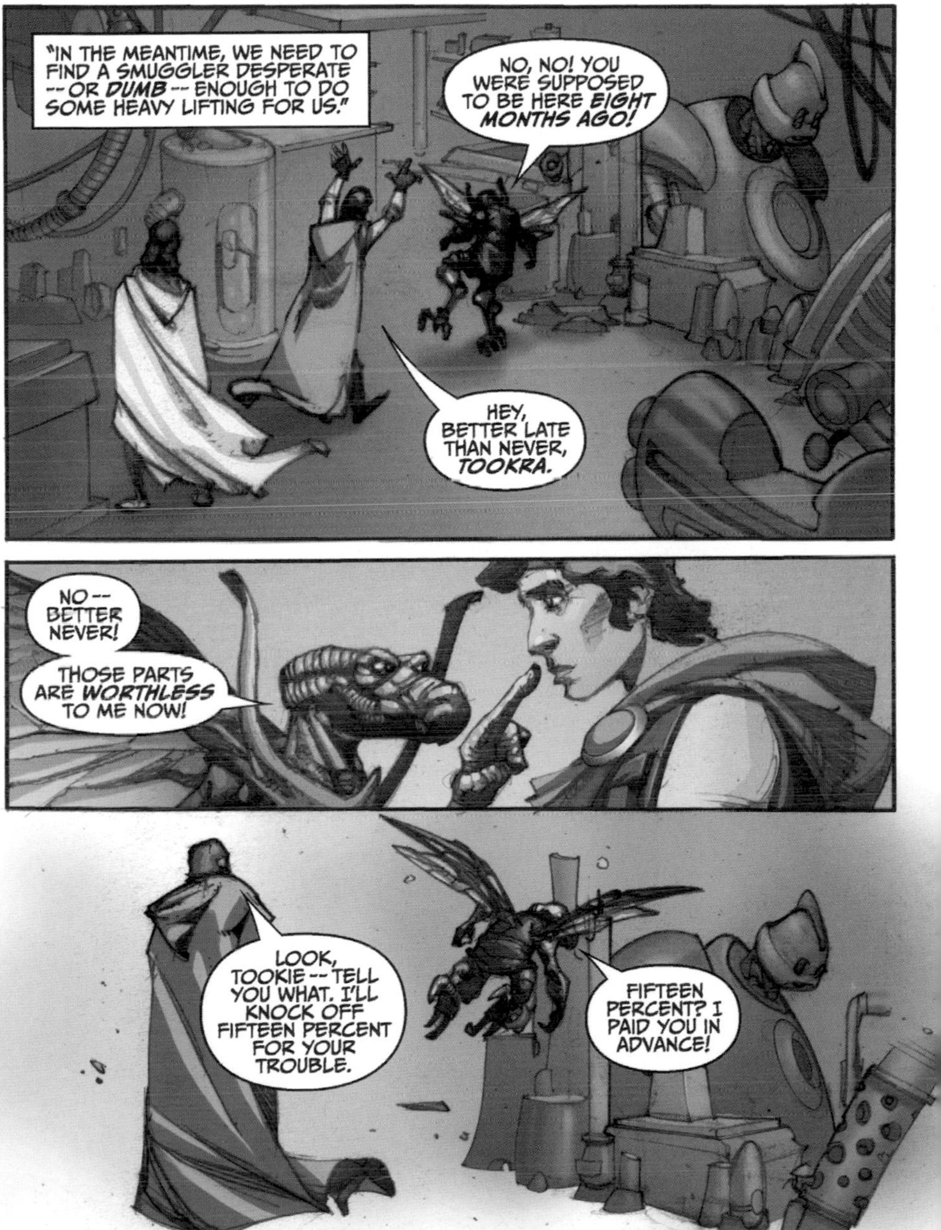
"IN THE MEANTIME, WE NEED TO FIND A SMUGGLER DESPERATE -- OR *DUMB* -- ENOUGH TO DO SOME HEAVY LIFTING FOR US."
NO, NO! YOU WERE SUPPOSED TO BE HERE *EIGHT MONTHS AGO!*
HEY, BETTER LATE THAN NEVER, *TOOKRA.*
NO -- BETTER NEVER!
THOSE PARTS ARE *WORTHLESS* TO ME NOW!
LOOK, TOOKIE -- TELL YOU WHAT. I'LL KNOCK OFF FIFTEEN PERCENT FOR YOUR TROUBLE.
FIFTEEN PERCENT? I PAID YOU IN ADVANCE!

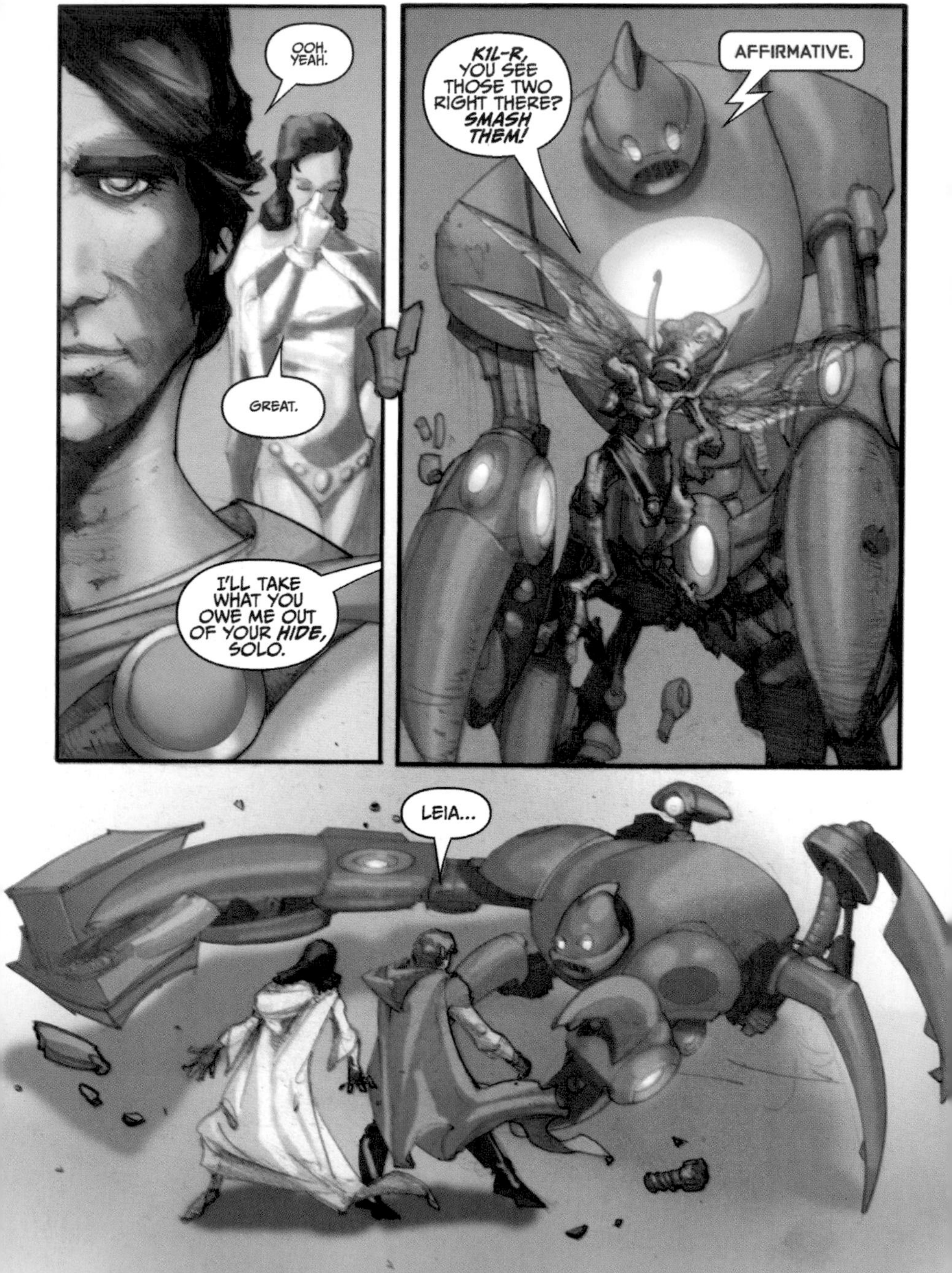
OOH. YEAH.
GREAT.
I'LL TAKE WHAT YOU OWE ME OUT OF YOUR HIDE, SOLO.
K1L-R, YOU SEE THOSE TWO RIGHT THERE? SMASH THEM!
AFFIRMATIVE.
LEIA...

[redacted]

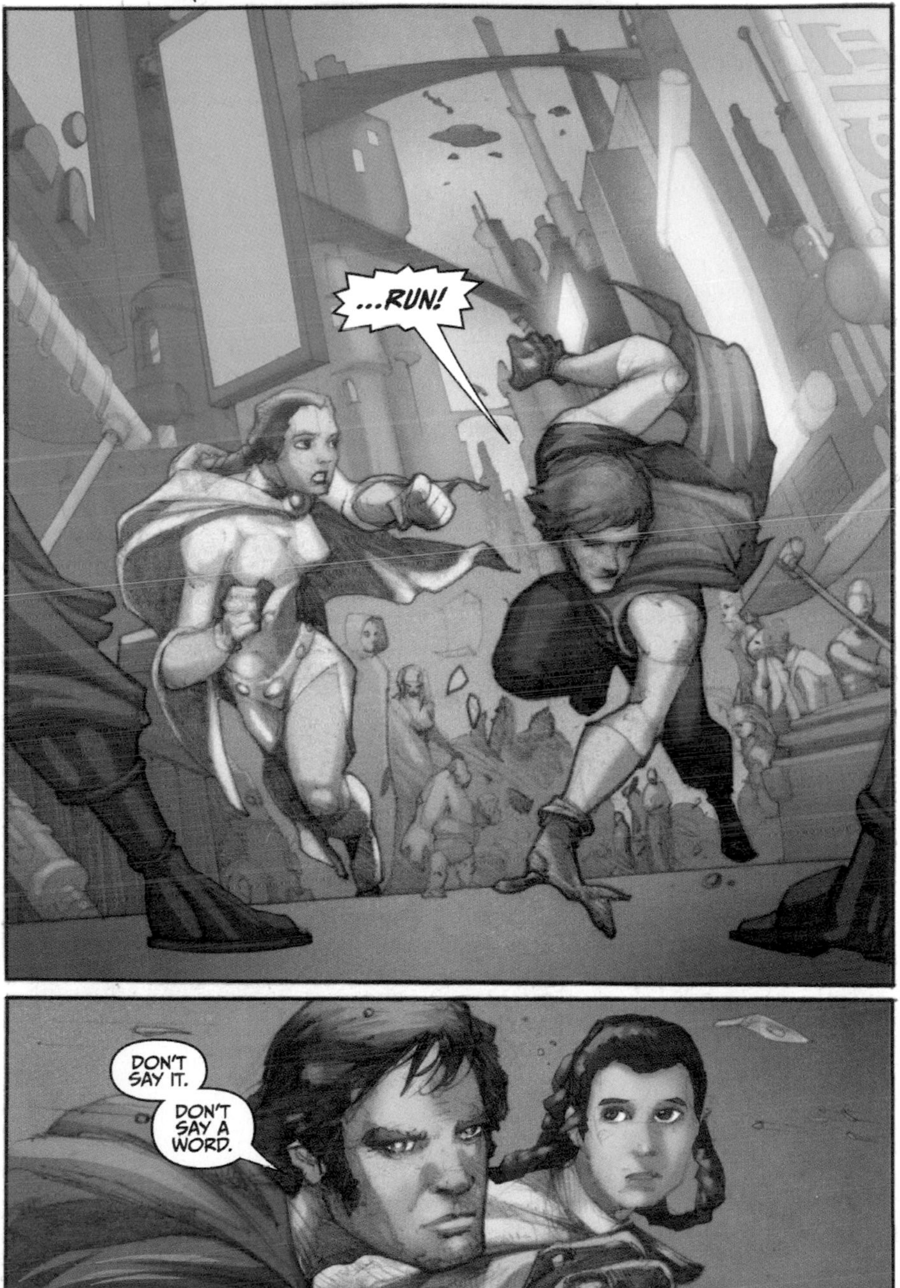
...RUN!
DON'T SAY IT.
DON'T SAY A WORD.

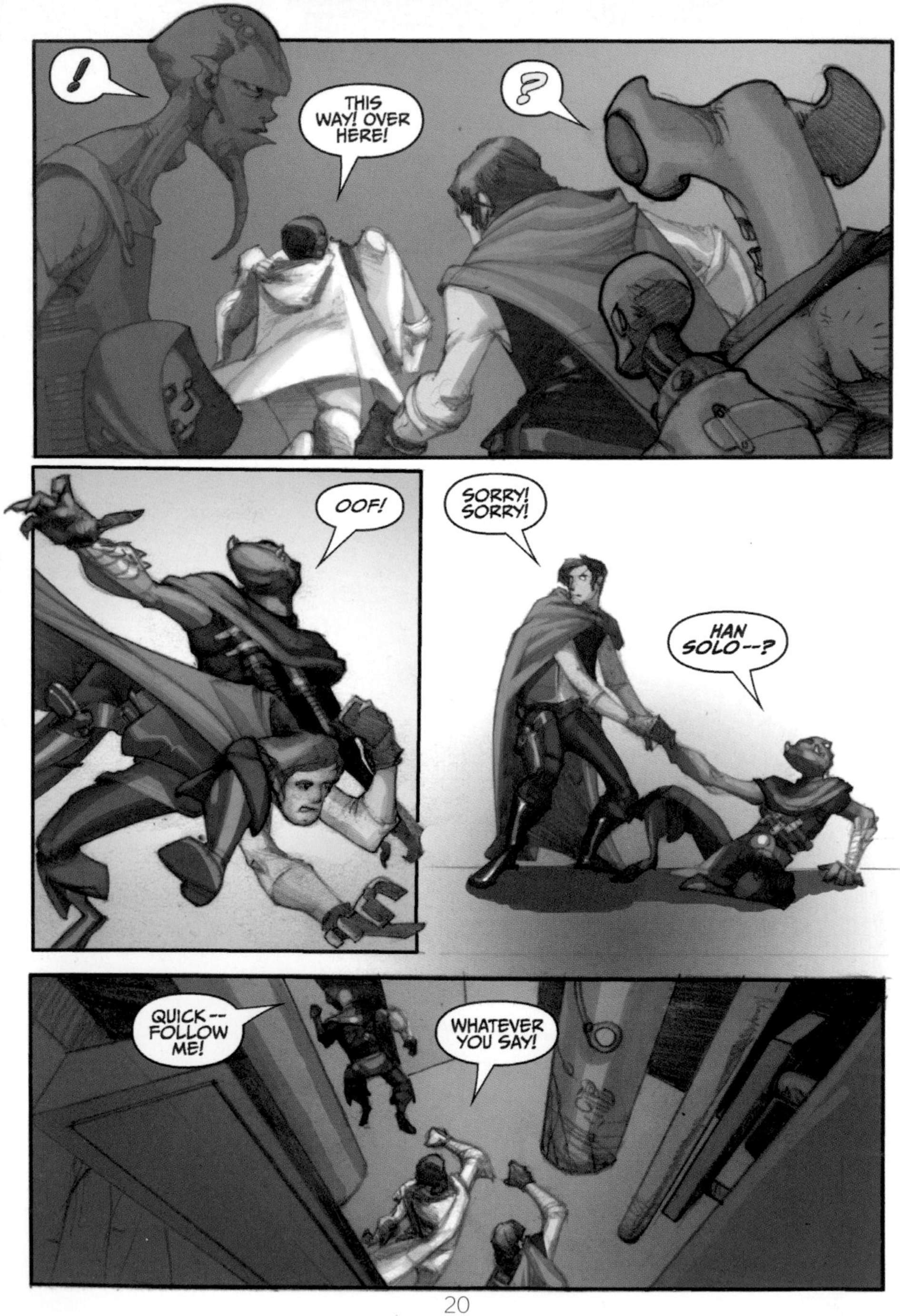
!
THIS WAY! OVER HERE!
?
OOF!
SORRY! SORRY!
HAN SOLO--?
QUICK--FOLLOW ME!
WHATEVER YOU SAY!

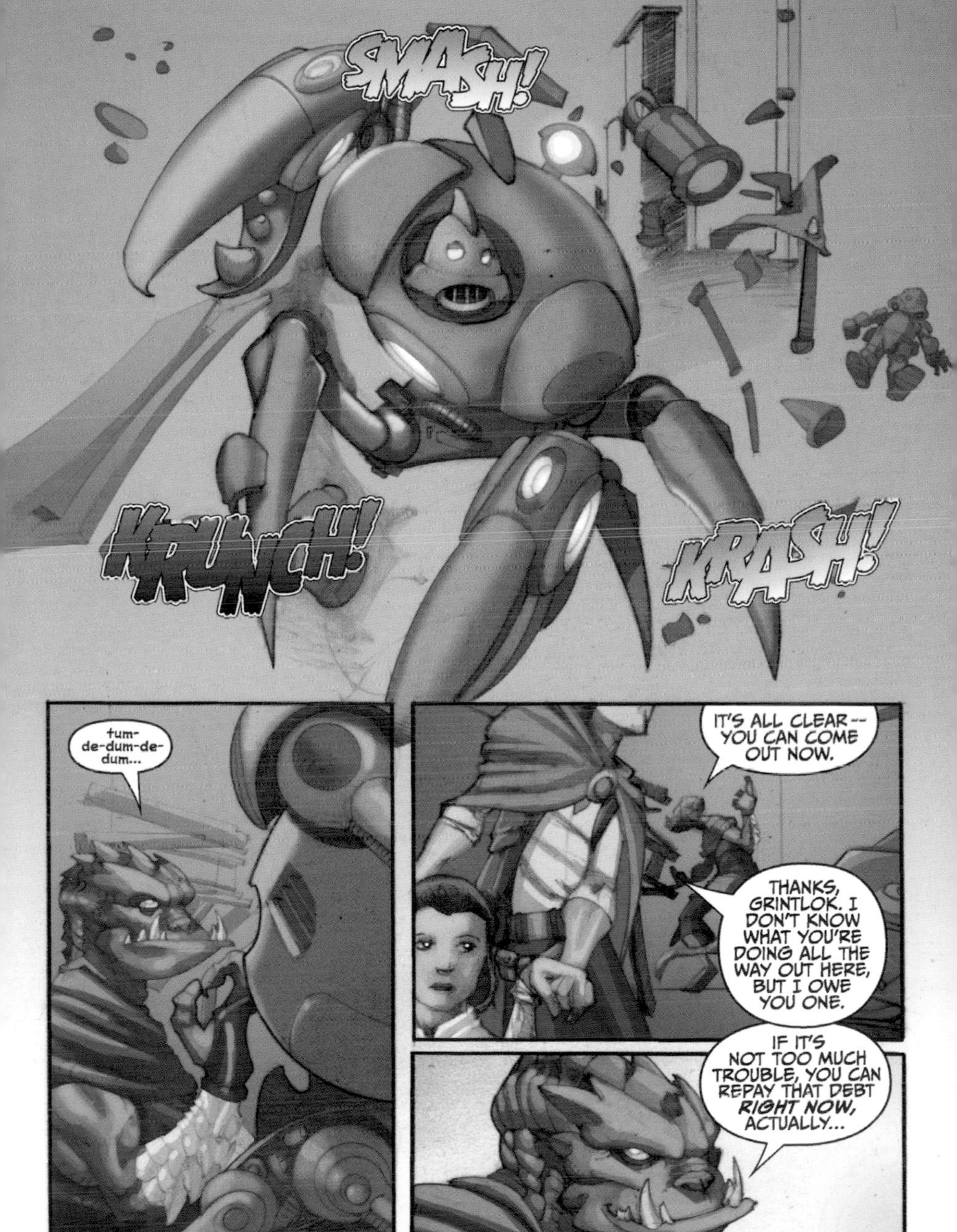
SMASH!
KRUNCH!
KRASH!
tum-de-dum-de-dum...
IT'S ALL CLEAR-- YOU CAN COME OUT NOW.
THANKS, GRINTLOK. I DON'T KNOW WHAT YOU'RE DOING ALL THE WAY OUT HERE, BUT I OWE YOU ONE.
IF IT'S NOT TOO MUCH TROUBLE, YOU CAN REPAY THAT DEBT *RIGHT NOW,* ACTUALLY...

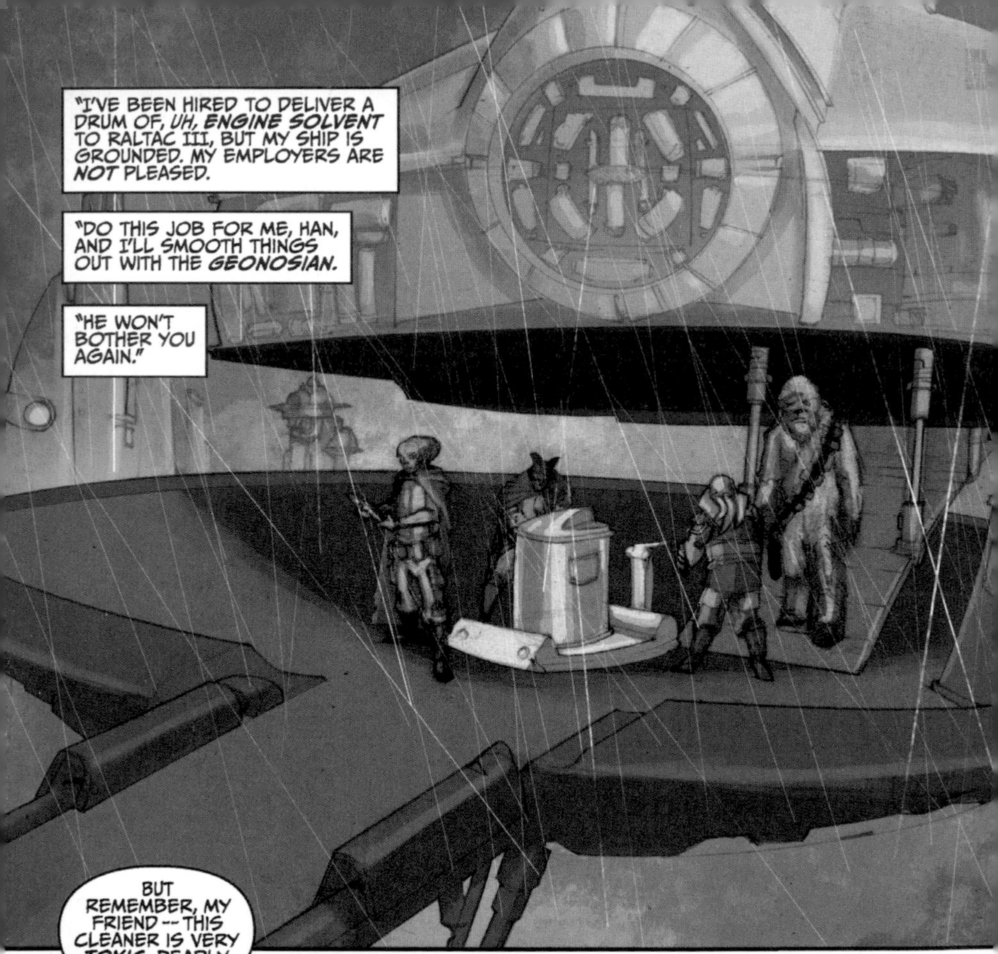
"I'VE BEEN HIRED TO DELIVER A DRUM OF, UH, ENGINE SOLVENT TO RALTAC III, BUT MY SHIP IS GROUNDED. MY EMPLOYERS ARE NOT PLEASED.
"DO THIS JOB FOR ME, HAN, AND I'LL SMOOTH THINGS OUT WITH THE GEONOSIAN.
"HE WON'T BOTHER YOU AGAIN."
BUT REMEMBER, MY FRIEND -- THIS CLEANER IS VERY TOXIC. DEADLY FUMES.

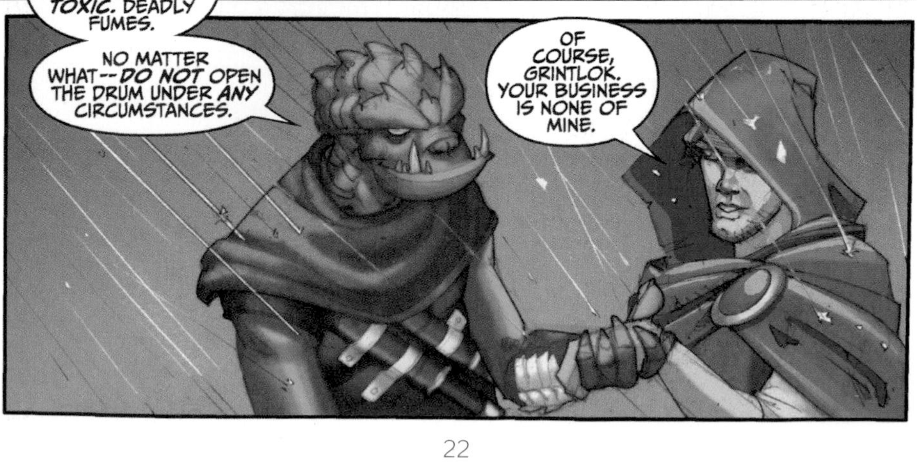
NO MATTER WHAT -- DO NOT OPEN THE DRUM UNDER ANY CIRCUMSTANCES.
OF COURSE, GRINTLOK. YOUR BUSINESS IS NONE OF MINE.

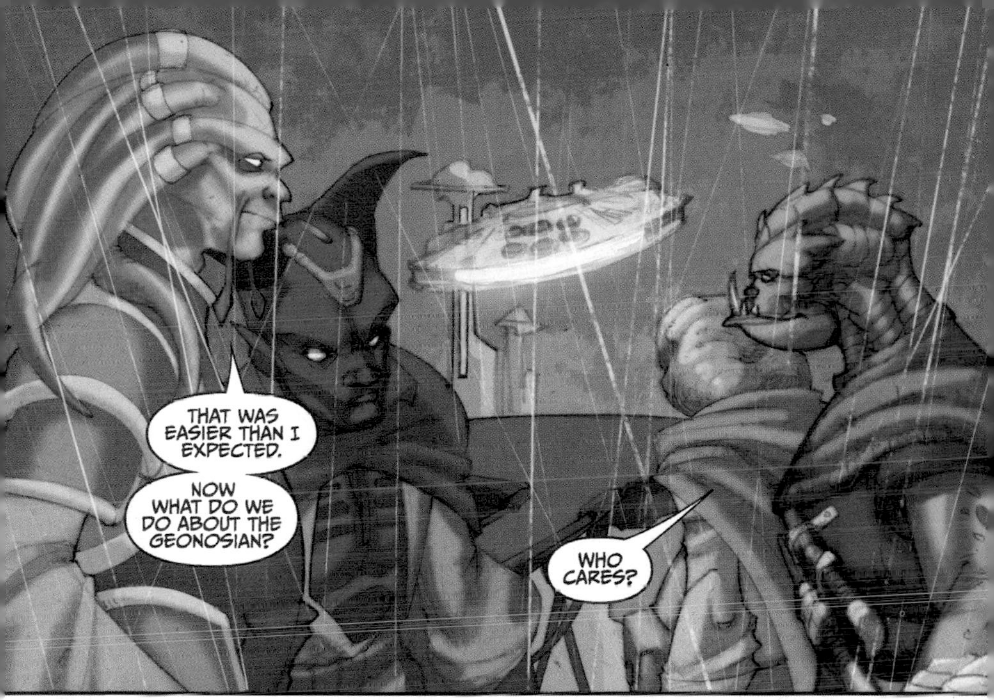
THAT WAS EASIER THAN I EXPECTED.
NOW WHAT DO WE DO ABOUT THE GEONOSIAN?
WHO CARES?

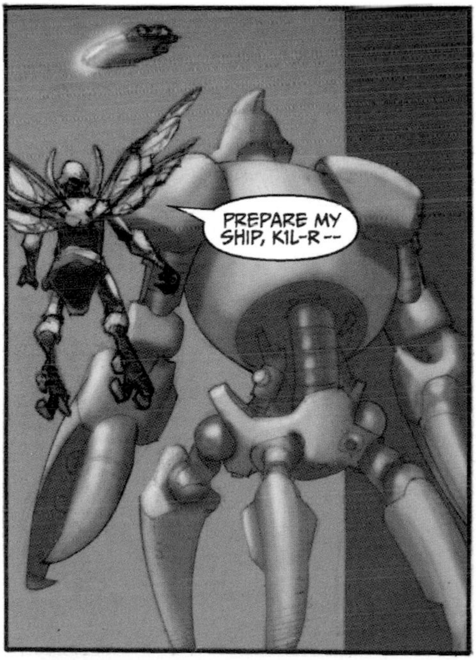
PREPARE MY SHIP, KIL-R --

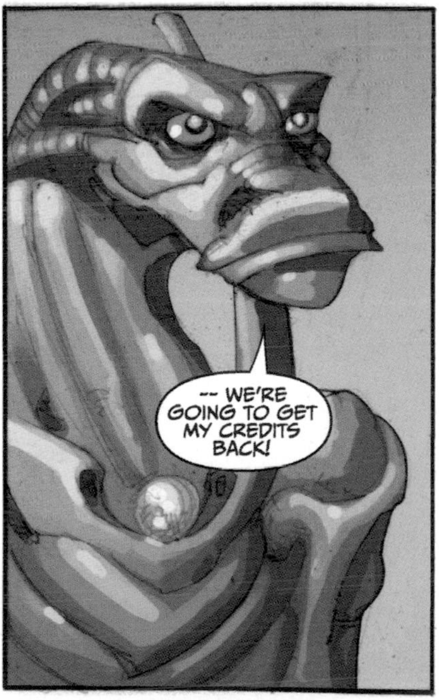
-- WE'RE GOING TO GET MY CREDITS BACK!

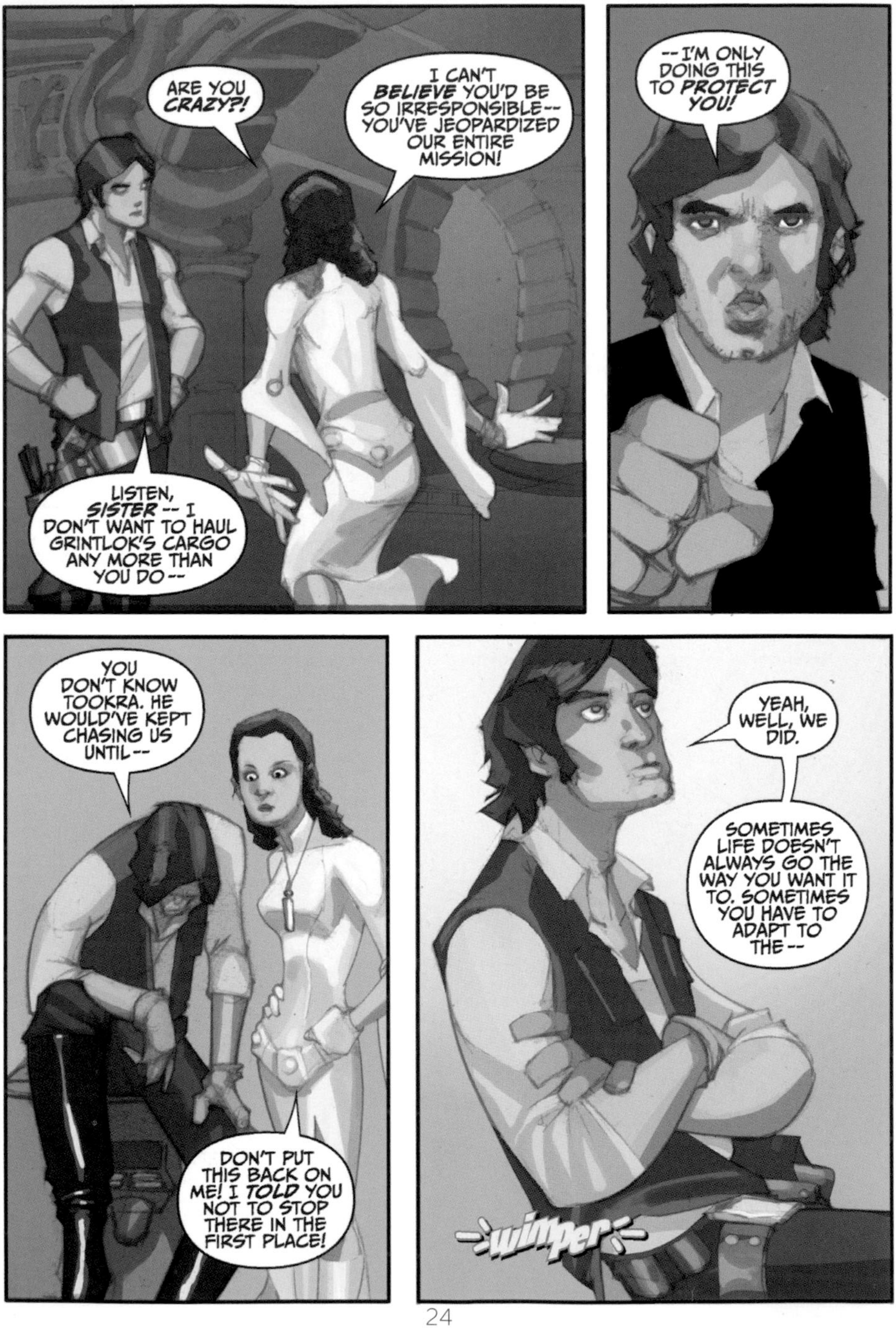
ARE YOU CRAZY?!
I CAN'T BELIEVE YOU'D BE SO IRRESPONSIBLE-- YOU'VE JEOPARDIZED OUR ENTIRE MISSION!
LISTEN, SISTER -- I DON'T WANT TO HAUL GRINTLOK'S CARGO ANY MORE THAN YOU DO--
--I'M ONLY DOING THIS TO PROTECT YOU!
YOU DON'T KNOW TOOKRA. HE WOULD'VE KEPT CHASING US UNTIL--
DON'T PUT THIS BACK ON ME! I TOLD YOU NOT TO STOP THERE IN THE FIRST PLACE!
YEAH, WELL, WE DID.
SOMETIMES LIFE DOESN'T ALWAYS GO THE WAY YOU WANT IT TO. SOMETIMES YOU HAVE TO ADAPT TO THE--
WIMPER

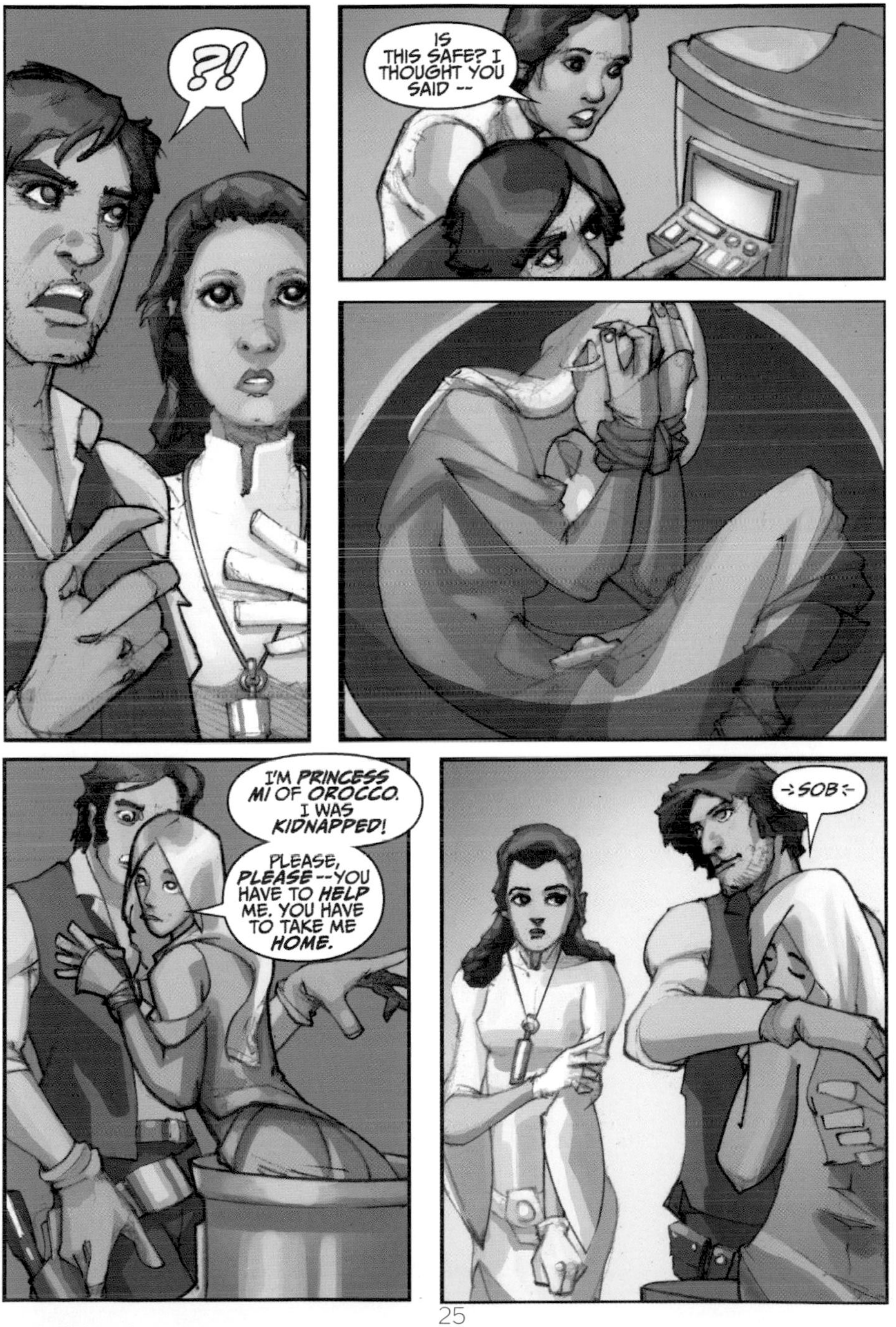

?!
IS THIS SAFE? I THOUGHT YOU SAID --
I'M PRINCESS MI OF OROCCO. I WAS KIDNAPPED!
PLEASE, PLEASE -- YOU HAVE TO HELP ME. YOU HAVE TO TAKE ME HOME.
SOB

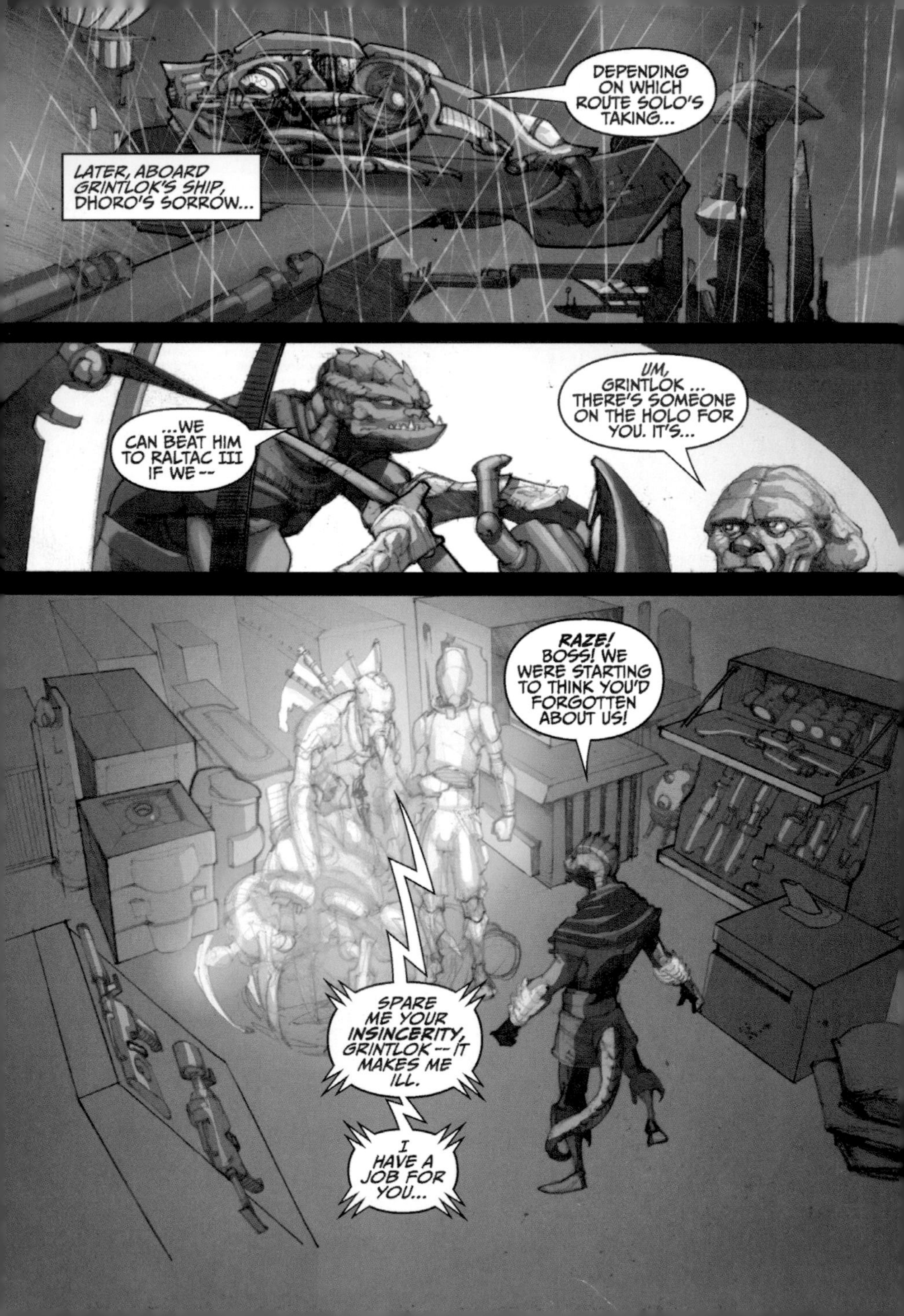

LATER, ABOARD GRINTLOK'S SHIP, DHORO'S SORROW...
DEPENDING ON WHICH ROUTE SOLO'S TAKING...
...WE CAN BEAT HIM TO RALTAC III IF WE--
UM, GRINTLOK ... THERE'S SOMEONE ON THE HOLO FOR YOU. IT'S...
RAZE! BOSS! WE WERE STARTING TO THINK YOU'D FORGOTTEN ABOUT US!
SPARE ME YOUR INSINCERITY, GRINTLOK -- IT MAKES ME ILL.
I HAVE A JOB FOR YOU...

...STUDY THIS STILL IMAGE. THIS IS PRINCESS MI OF OROCCO.

SHE'S THE DAUGHTER OF A VERY IMPORTANT FRIEND OF MINE AND SHE HAS BEEN KIDNAPPED.

THERE HAVE BEEN RANSOM DEMANDS. HER FATHER IS FRANTIC AND HE CAME TO ME FOR HELP.

SO NOW I'M COMING TO YOU...

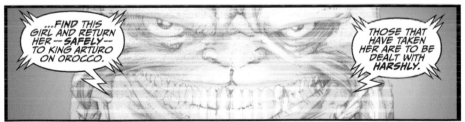

...FIND THIS GIRL AND RETURN HER--SAFELY--TO KING ARTURO ON OROCCO.

THOSE THAT HAVE TAKEN HER ARE TO BE DEALT WITH HARSHLY.

CONTRACT ACCEPTED.

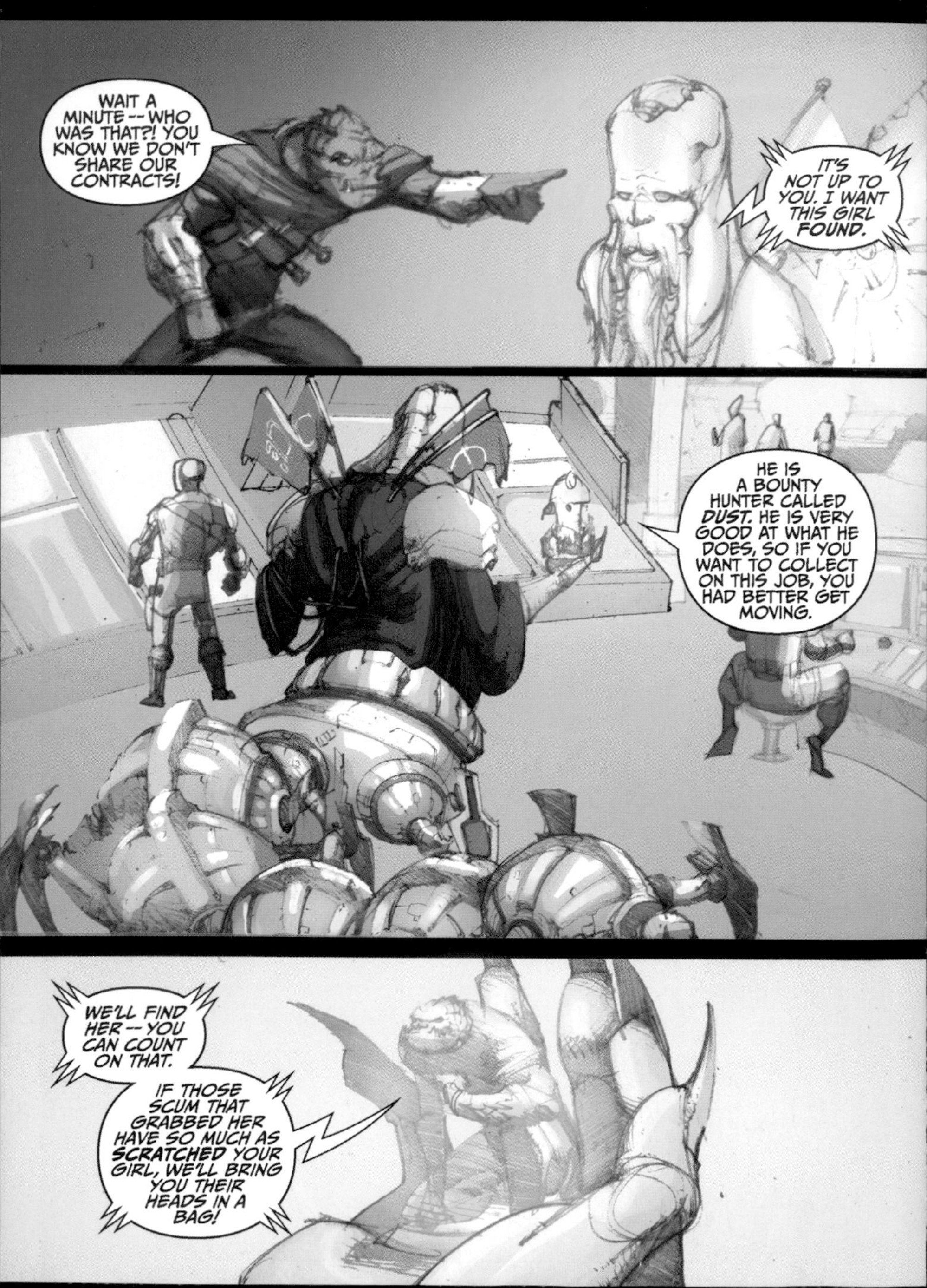
WAIT A MINUTE -- WHO WAS THAT?! YOU KNOW WE DON'T SHARE OUR CONTRACTS!
IT'S NOT UP TO YOU. I WANT THIS GIRL FOUND.
HE IS A BOUNTY HUNTER CALLED DUST. HE IS VERY GOOD AT WHAT HE DOES, SO IF YOU WANT TO COLLECT ON THIS JOB, YOU HAD BETTER GET MOVING.
WE'LL FIND HER -- YOU CAN COUNT ON THAT.
IF THOSE SCUM THAT GRABBED HER HAVE SO MUCH AS SCRATCHED YOUR GIRL, WE'LL BRING YOU THEIR HEADS IN A BAG!

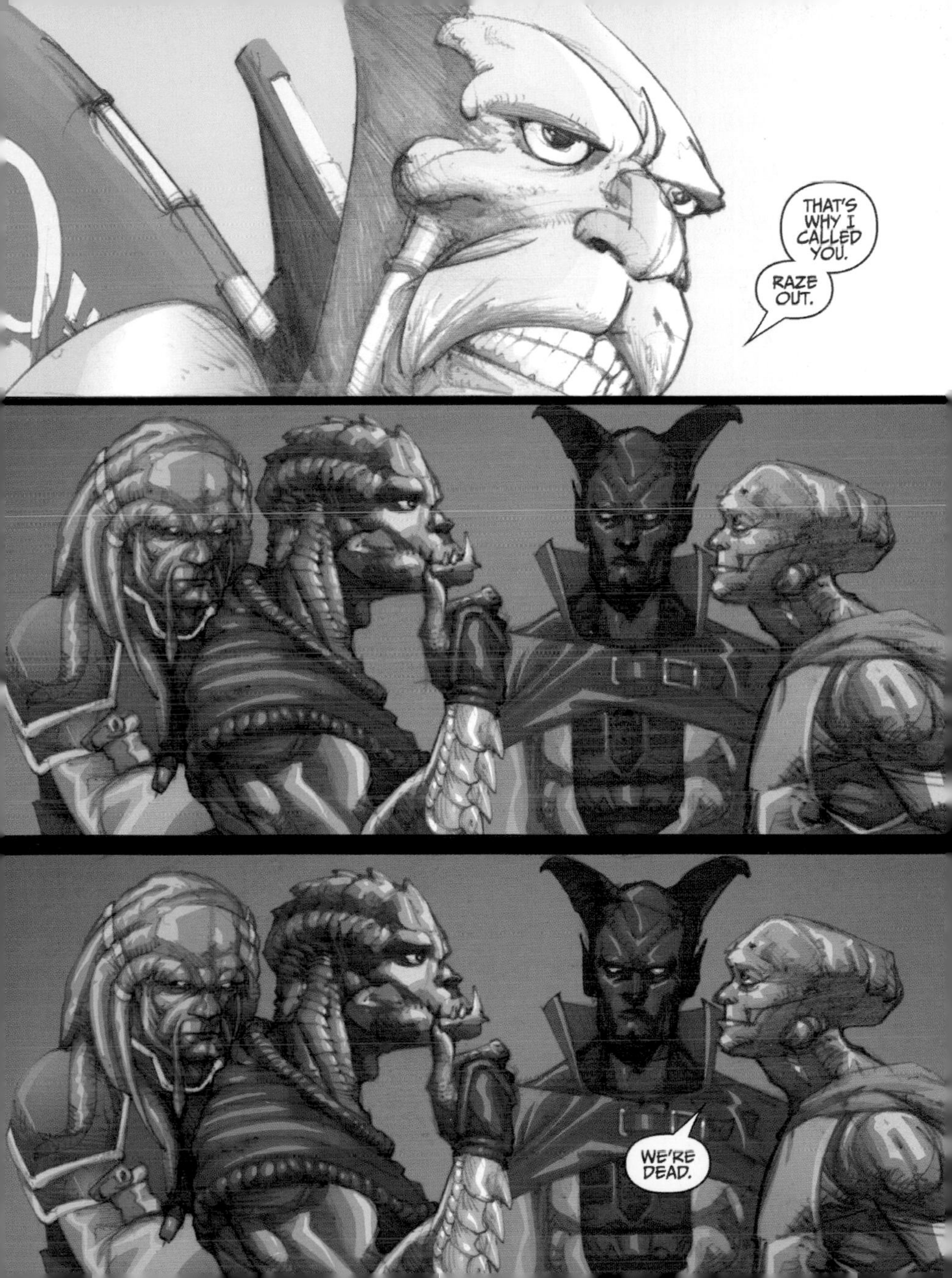
THAT'S WHY I CALLED YOU.
RAZE OUT.
WE'RE DEAD.

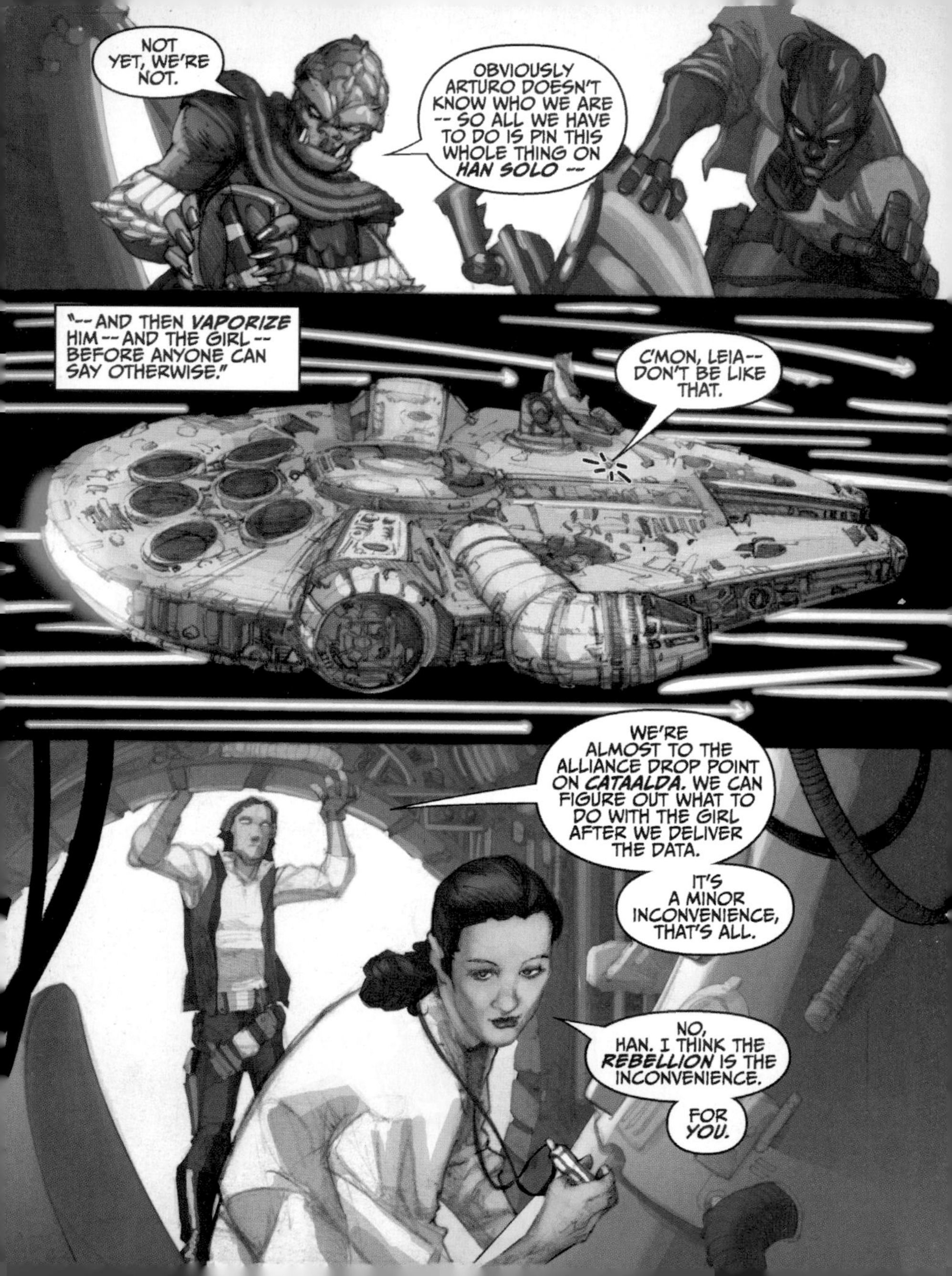
NOT YET, WE'RE NOT.
OBVIOUSLY ARTURO DOESN'T KNOW WHO WE ARE -- SO ALL WE HAVE TO DO IS PIN THIS WHOLE THING ON HAN SOLO --
"-- AND THEN VAPORIZE HIM -- AND THE GIRL -- BEFORE ANYONE CAN SAY OTHERWISE."
C'MON, LEIA-- DON'T BE LIKE THAT.
WE'RE ALMOST TO THE ALLIANCE DROP POINT ON CATAALDA. WE CAN FIGURE OUT WHAT TO DO WITH THE GIRL AFTER WE DELIVER THE DATA.
IT'S A MINOR INCONVENIENCE, THAT'S ALL.
NO, HAN. I THINK THE REBELLION IS THE INCONVENIENCE.
FOR YOU.

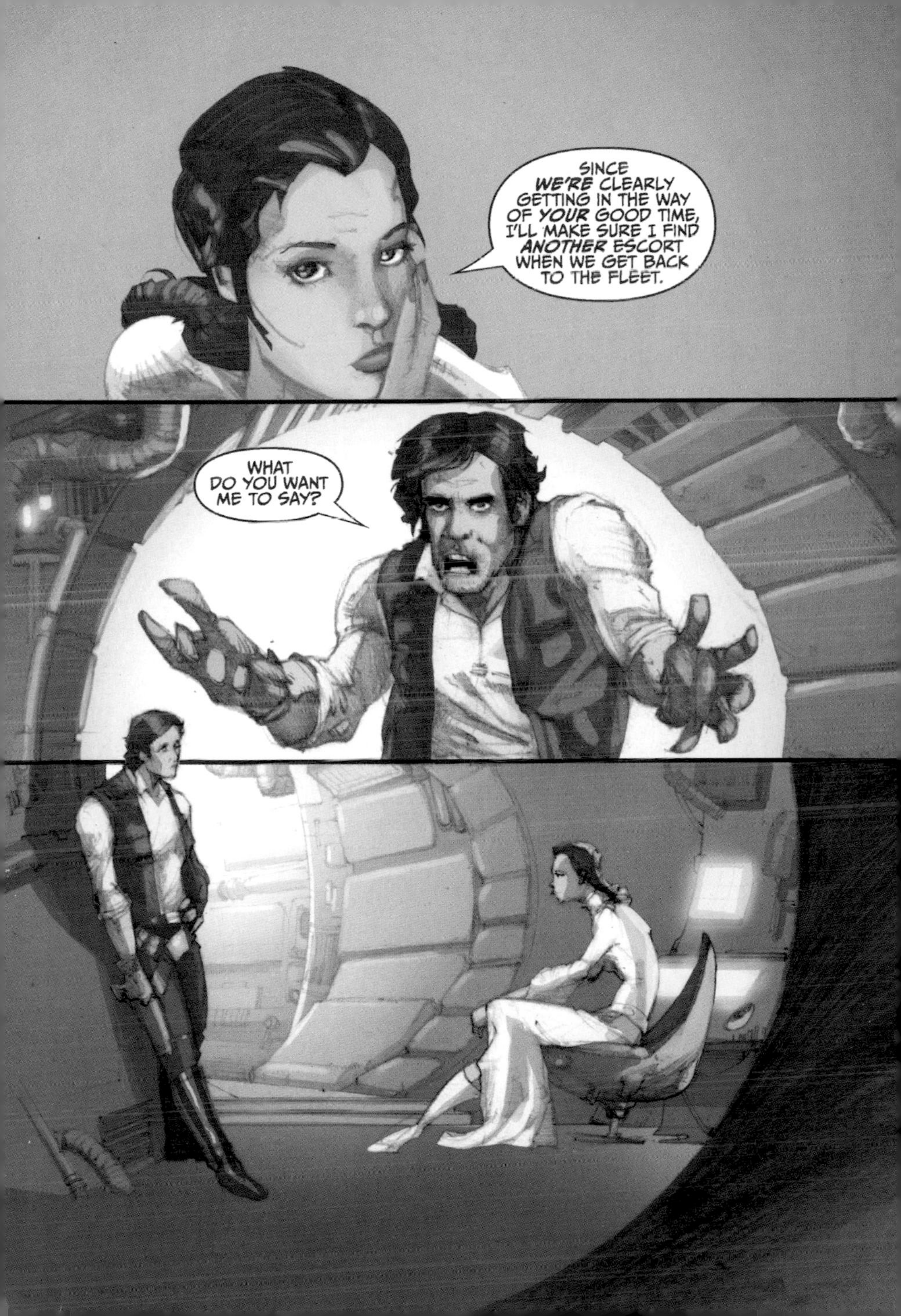
SINCE WE'RE CLEARLY GETTING IN THE WAY OF YOUR GOOD TIME, I'LL MAKE SURE I FIND ANOTHER ESCORT WHEN WE GET BACK TO THE FLEET.
WHAT DO YOU WANT ME TO SAY?

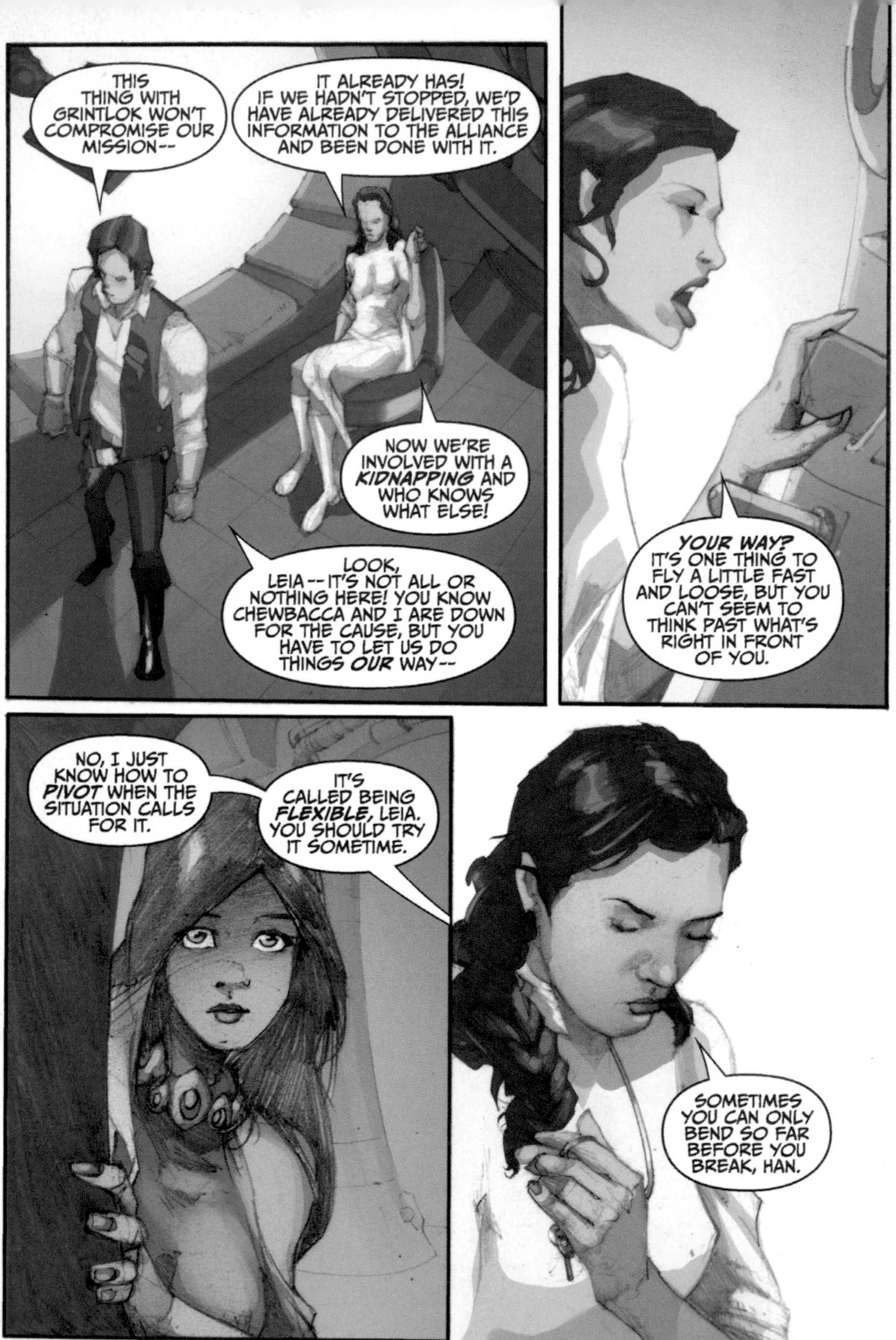
THIS THING WITH GRINTLOK WON'T COMPROMISE OUR MISSION--
IT ALREADY HAS! IF WE HADN'T STOPPED, WE'D HAVE ALREADY DELIVERED THIS INFORMATION TO THE ALLIANCE AND BEEN DONE WITH IT.
NOW WE'RE INVOLVED WITH A KIDNAPPING AND WHO KNOWS WHAT ELSE!
LOOK, LEIA--IT'S NOT ALL OR NOTHING HERE! YOU KNOW CHEWBACCA AND I ARE DOWN FOR THE CAUSE, BUT YOU HAVE TO LET US DO THINGS OUR WAY--
YOUR WAY? IT'S ONE THING TO FLY A LITTLE FAST AND LOOSE, BUT YOU CAN'T SEEM TO THINK PAST WHAT'S RIGHT IN FRONT OF YOU.
NO, I JUST KNOW HOW TO PIVOT WHEN THE SITUATION CALLS FOR IT.
IT'S CALLED BEING FLEXIBLE, LEIA. YOU SHOULD TRY IT SOMETIME.
SOMETIMES YOU CAN ONLY BEND SO FAR BEFORE YOU BREAK, HAN.

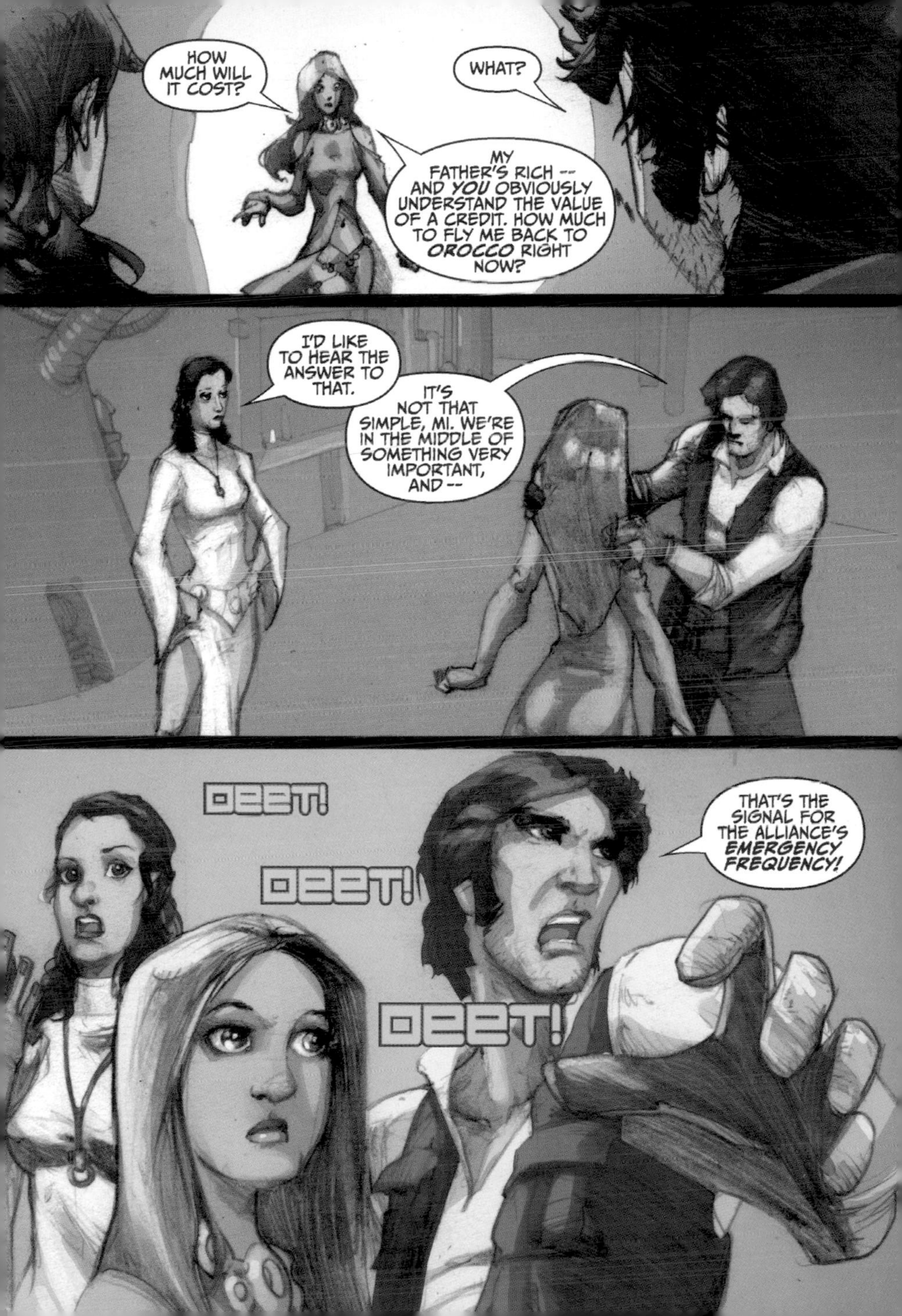
HOW MUCH WILL IT COST?
WHAT?
MY FATHER'S RICH -- AND *YOU* OBVIOUSLY UNDERSTAND THE VALUE OF A CREDIT. HOW MUCH TO FLY ME BACK TO *OROCCO* RIGHT NOW?
I'D LIKE TO HEAR THE ANSWER TO THAT.
IT'S NOT THAT SIMPLE, MI. WE'RE IN THE MIDDLE OF SOMETHING VERY IMPORTANT, AND --
DEET!
DEET!
DEET!
THAT'S THE SIGNAL FOR THE ALLIANCE'S *EMERGENCY FREQUENCY!*

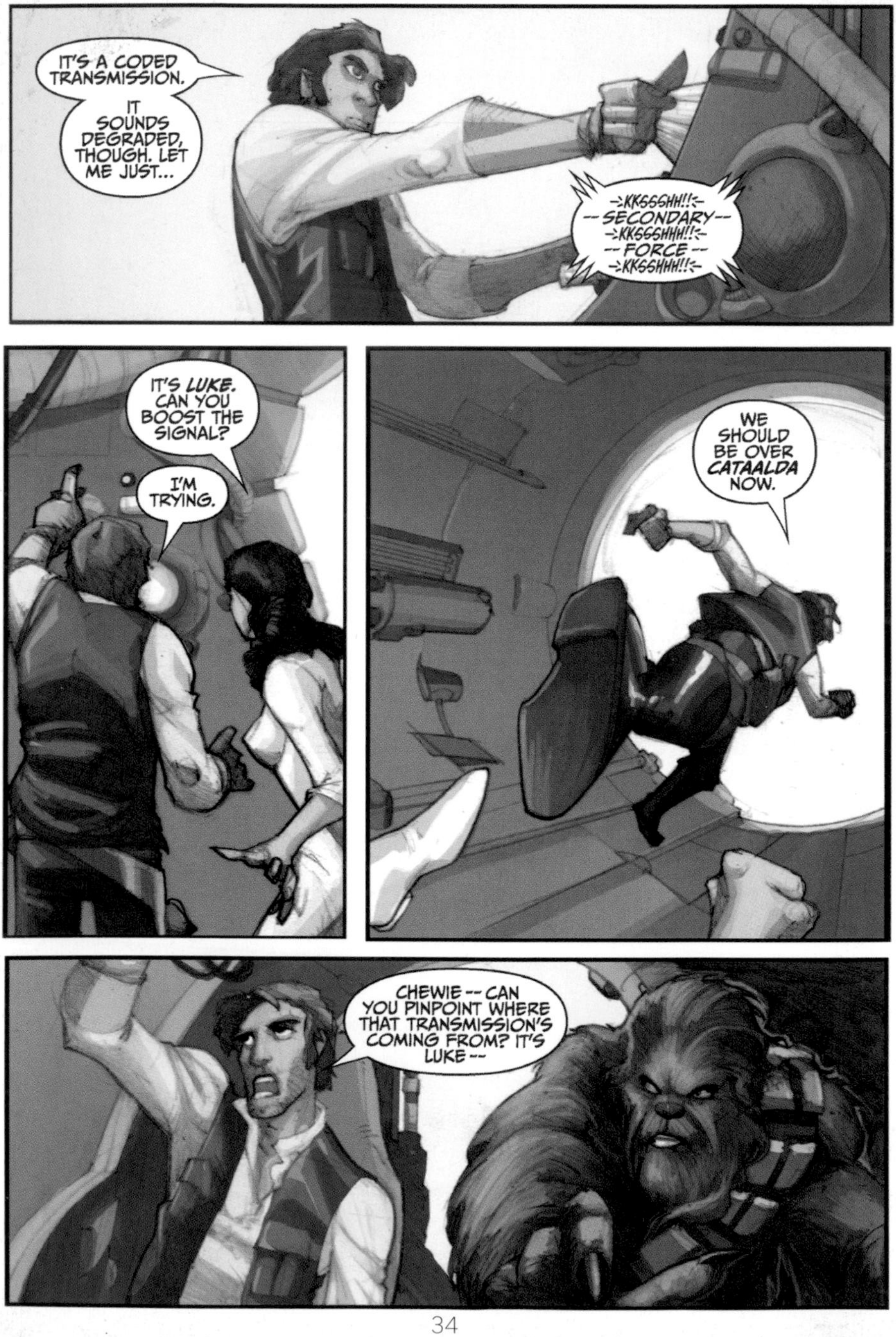
IT'S A CODED TRANSMISSION.
IT SOUNDS DEGRADED, THOUGH. LET ME JUST...
-KKSSSHH!!- --SECONDARY-- -KKSSSHHH!!- --FORCE-- -KKSSHHH!!-
IT'S LUKE. CAN YOU BOOST THE SIGNAL?
I'M TRYING.
WE SHOULD BE OVER CATAALDA NOW.
CHEWIE -- CAN YOU PINPOINT WHERE THAT TRANSMISSION'S COMING FROM? IT'S LUKE --

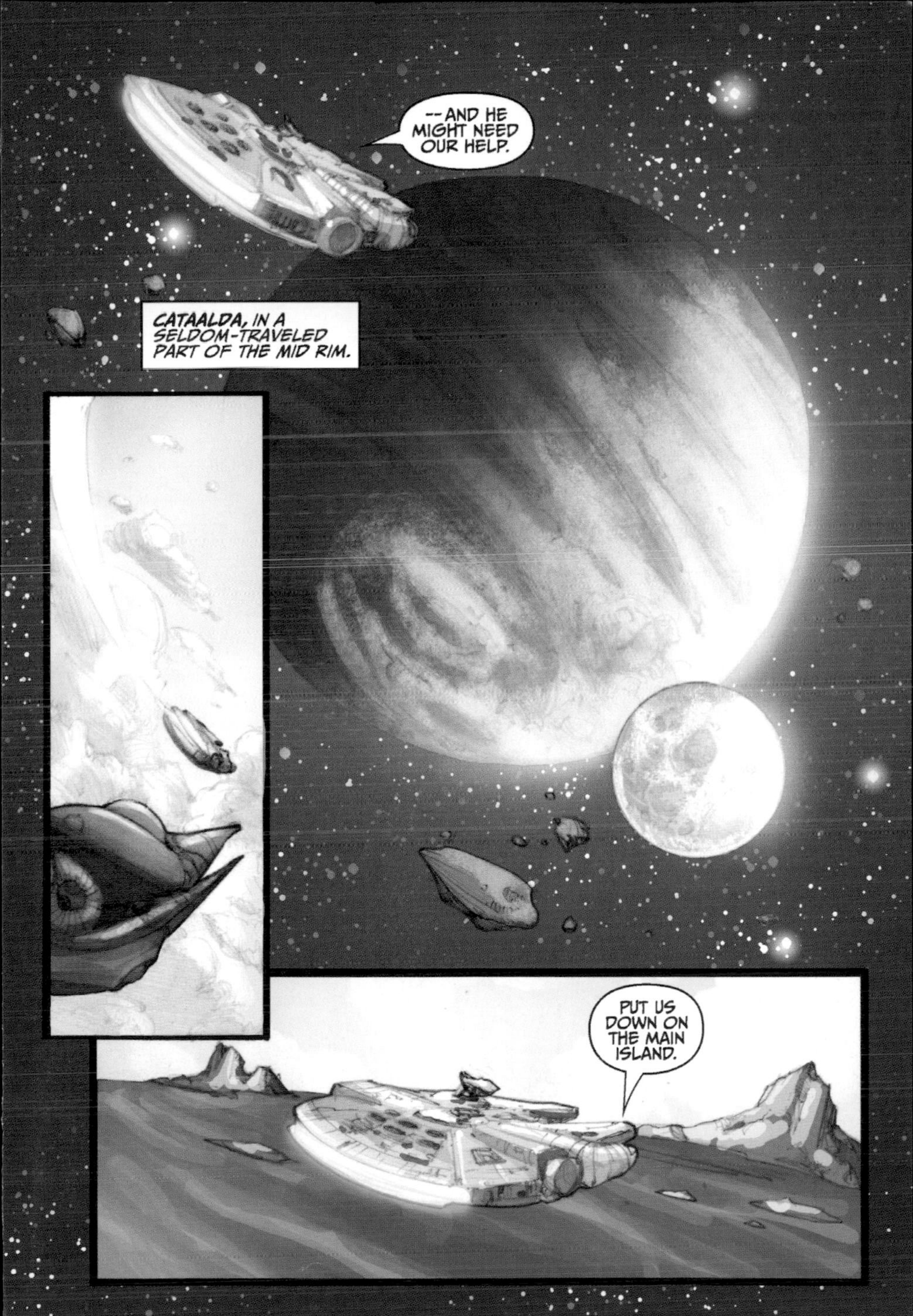
--AND HE MIGHT NEED OUR HELP.
CATAALDA, IN A SELDOM-TRAVELED PART OF THE MID RIM.
PUT US DOWN ON THE MAIN ISLAND.

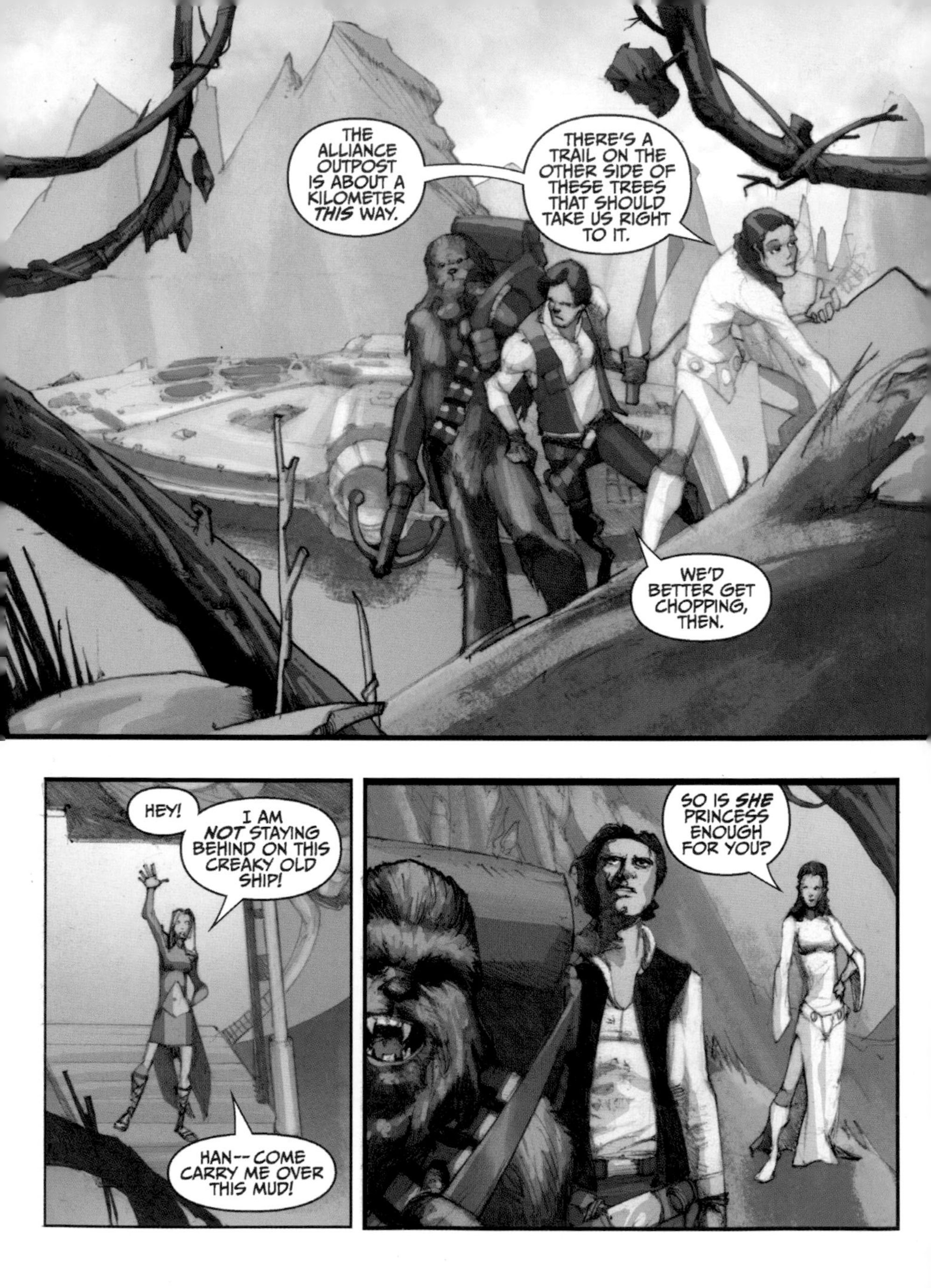
THE ALLIANCE OUTPOST IS ABOUT A KILOMETER *THIS* WAY.
THERE'S A TRAIL ON THE OTHER SIDE OF THESE TREES THAT SHOULD TAKE US RIGHT TO IT.
WE'D BETTER GET CHOPPING, THEN.
HEY!
I AM *NOT* STAYING BEHIND ON THIS CREAKY OLD SHIP!
HAN--COME CARRY ME OVER THIS MUD!
SO IS *SHE* PRINCESS ENOUGH FOR YOU?

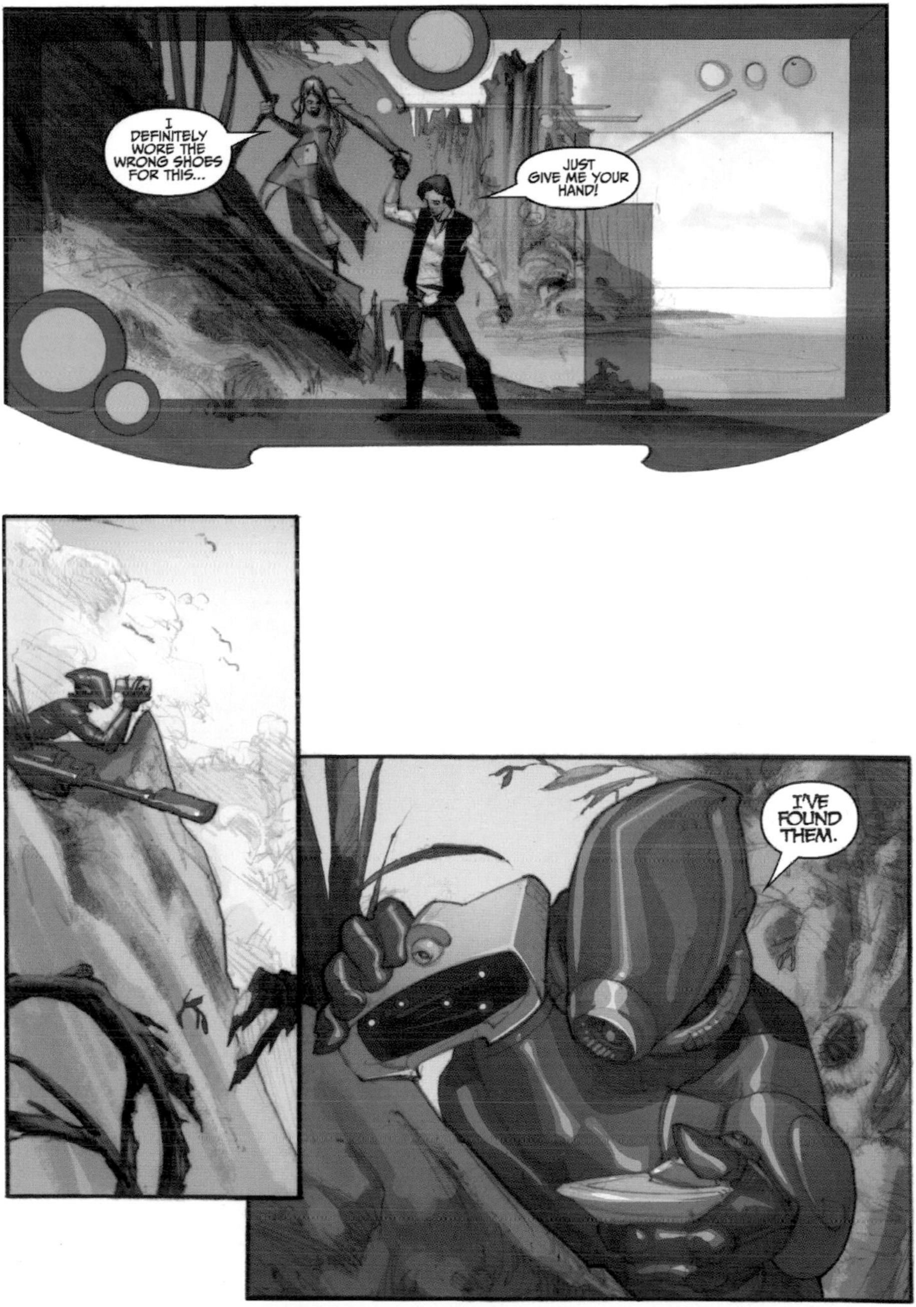
I DEFINITELY WORE THE WRONG SHOES FOR THIS...
JUST GIVE ME YOUR HAND!
I'VE FOUND THEM.

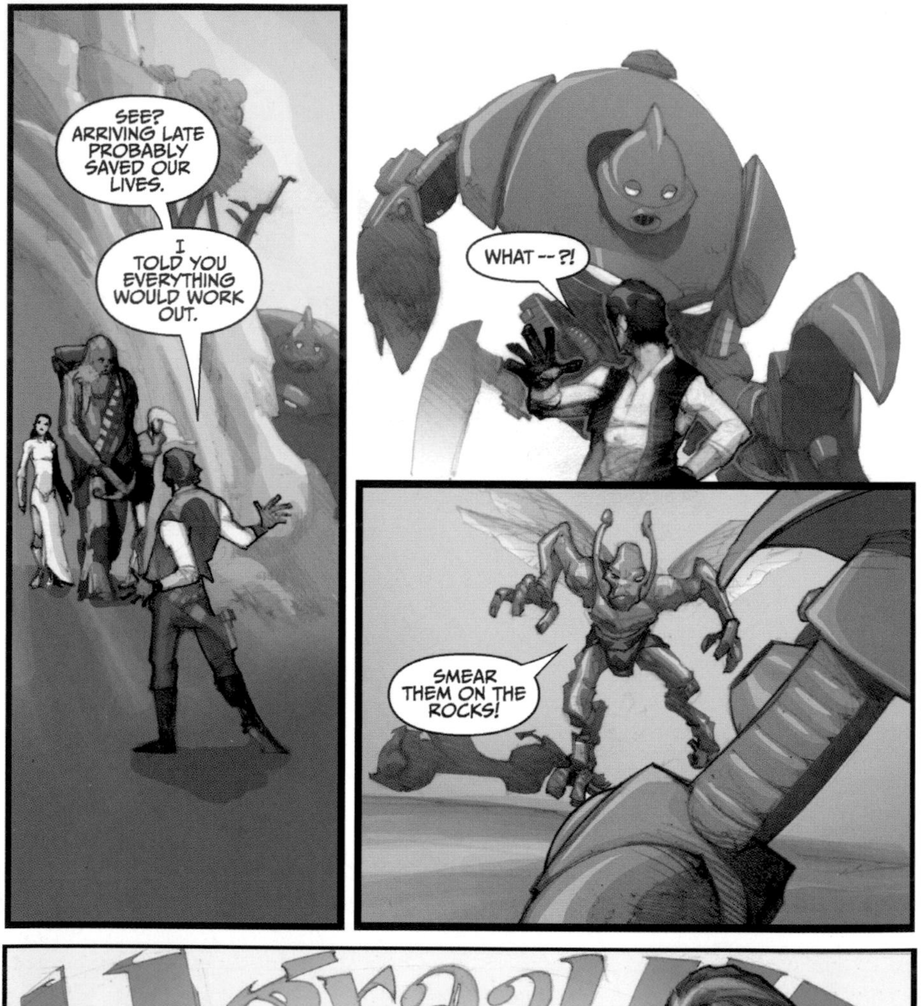
SEE? ARRIVING LATE PROBABLY SAVED OUR LIVES.
I TOLD YOU EVERYTHING WOULD WORK OUT.
WHAT -- ?!
SMEAR THEM ON THE ROCKS!

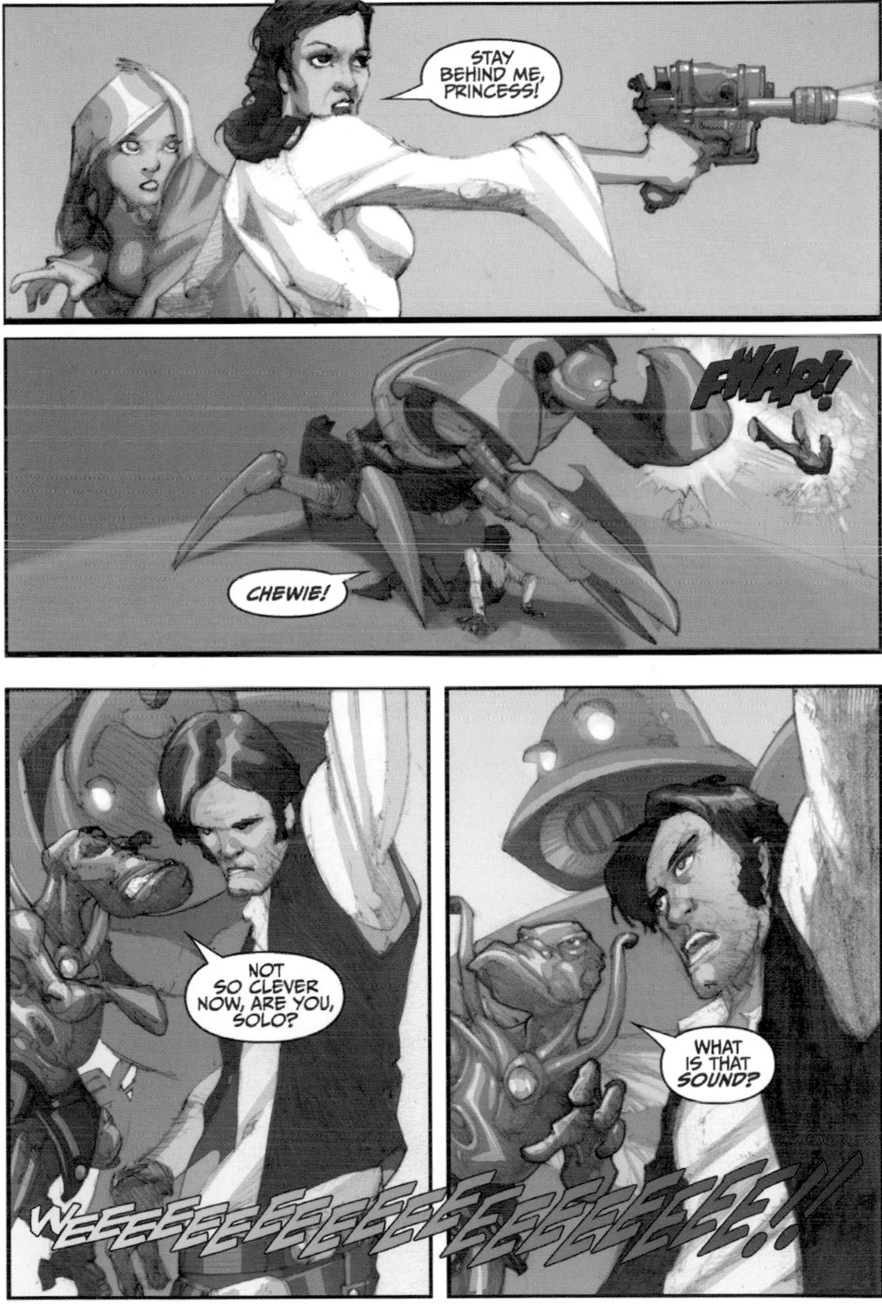
STAY BEHIND ME, PRINCESS!
FWAP!!
CHEWIE!
NOT SO CLEVER NOW, ARE YOU, SOLO?
WHAT IS THAT SOUND?
WEEEEEEEEEEEEEEEEEEEEEEEEEE!!

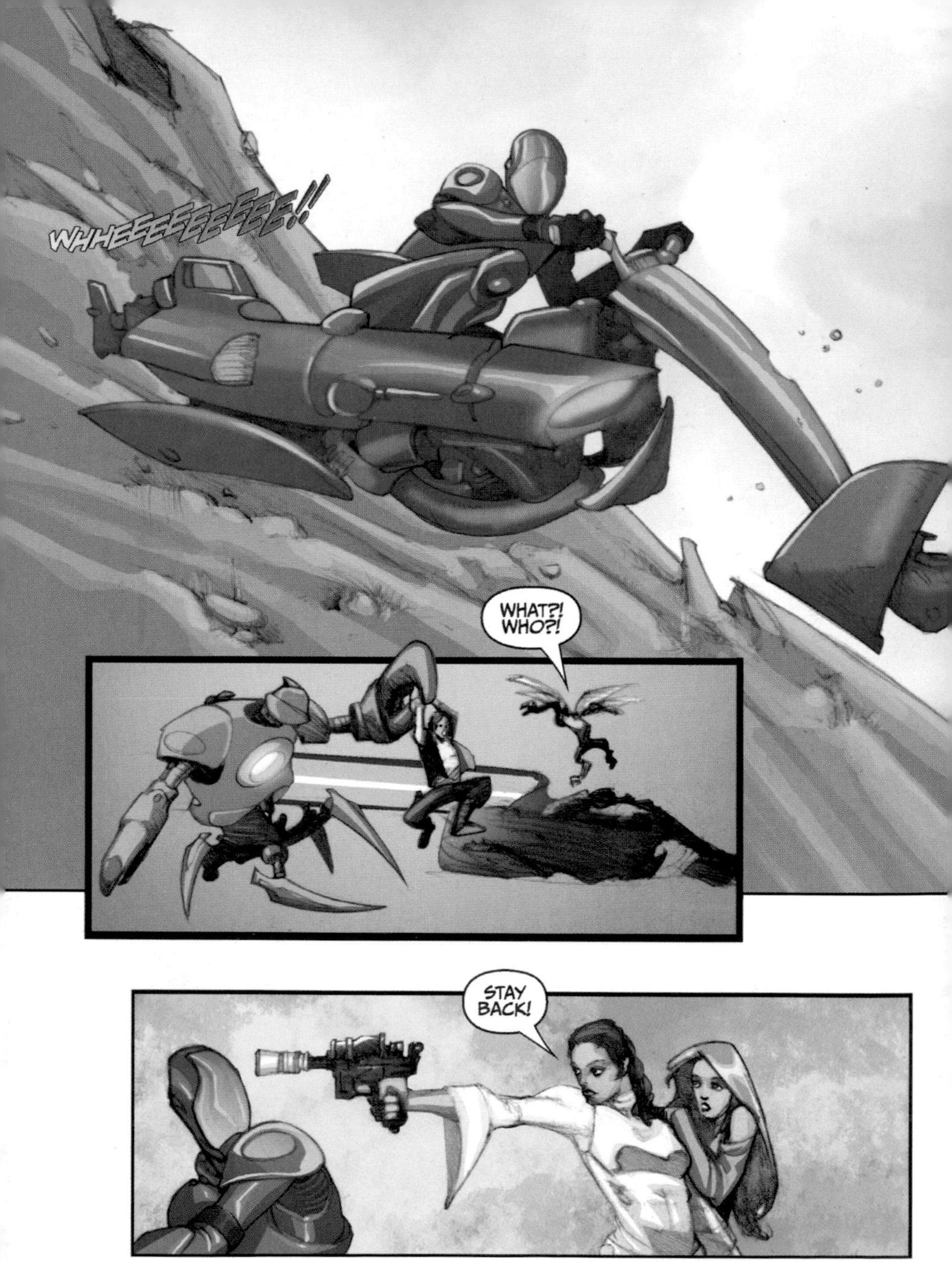
WHHEEEEEEEEEEE!!
WHAT?! WHO?!
STAY BACK!

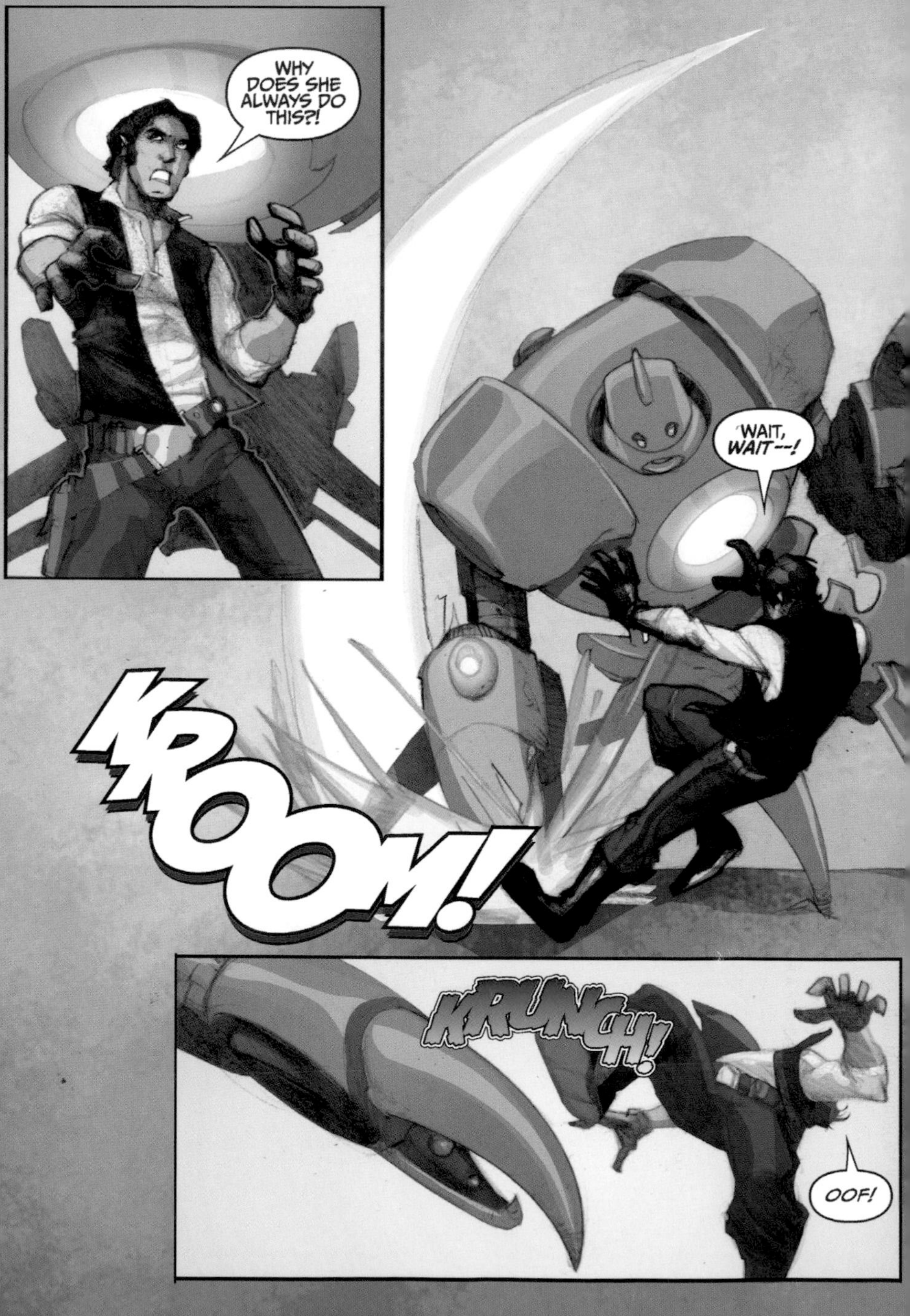
WHY DOES SHE ALWAYS DO THIS?!
WAIT, WAIT--!
KROOOM!
KRUNCH!
OOF!

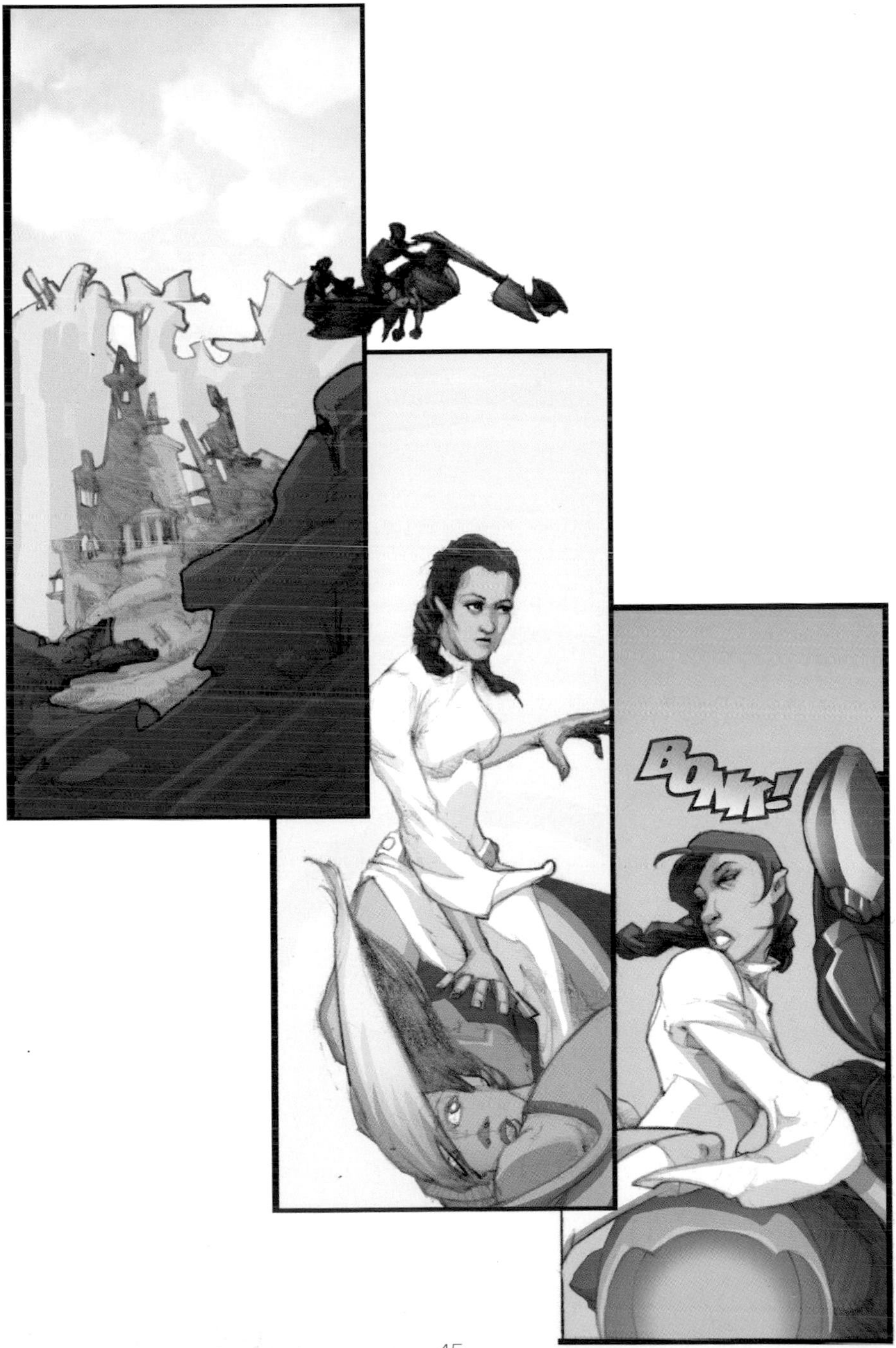
BONK!

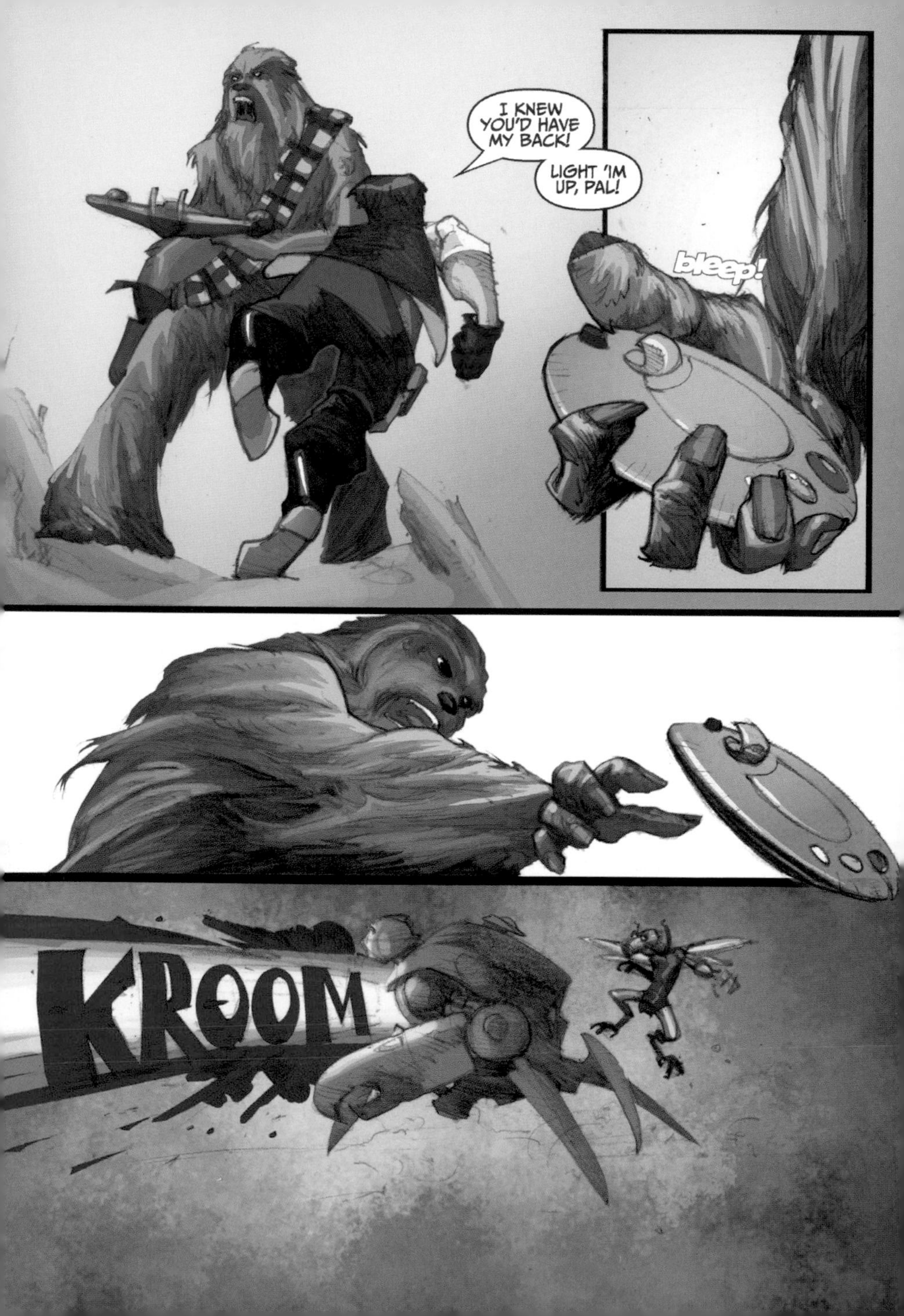
I KNEW YOU'D HAVE MY BACK!
LIGHT 'IM UP, PAL!
bleep!
KROOM

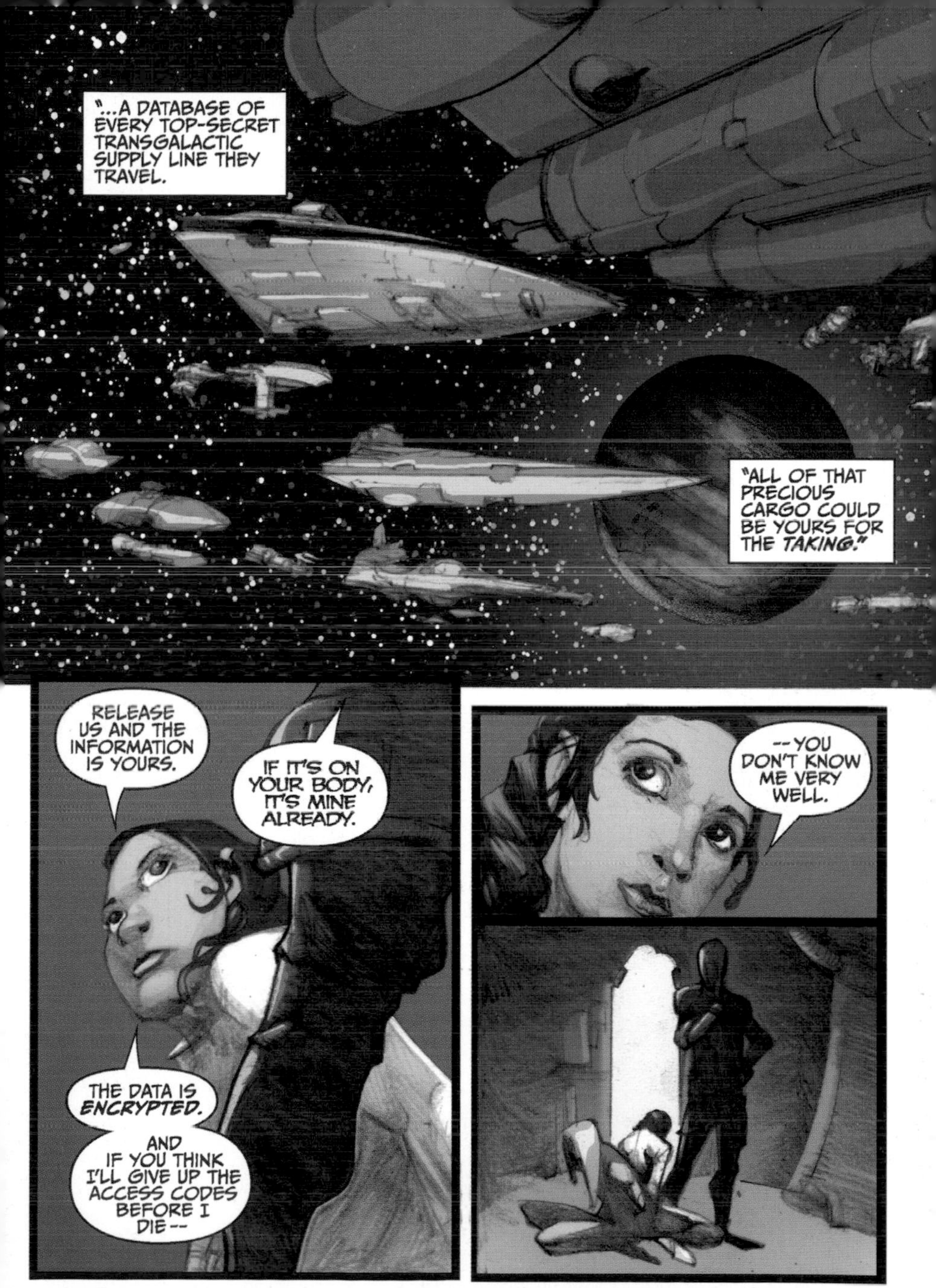
"...A DATABASE OF EVERY TOP-SECRET TRANSGALACTIC SUPPLY LINE THEY TRAVEL.
"ALL OF THAT PRECIOUS CARGO COULD BE YOURS FOR THE *TAKING*."
RELEASE US AND THE INFORMATION IS YOURS.
IF IT'S ON YOUR BODY, IT'S MINE ALREADY.
THE DATA IS *ENCRYPTED*.
AND IF YOU THINK I'LL GIVE UP THE ACCESS CODES BEFORE I DIE--
--YOU DON'T KNOW ME VERY WELL.

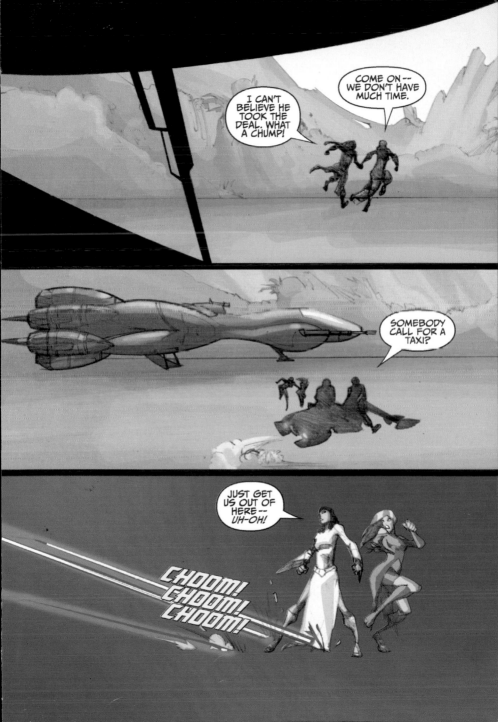

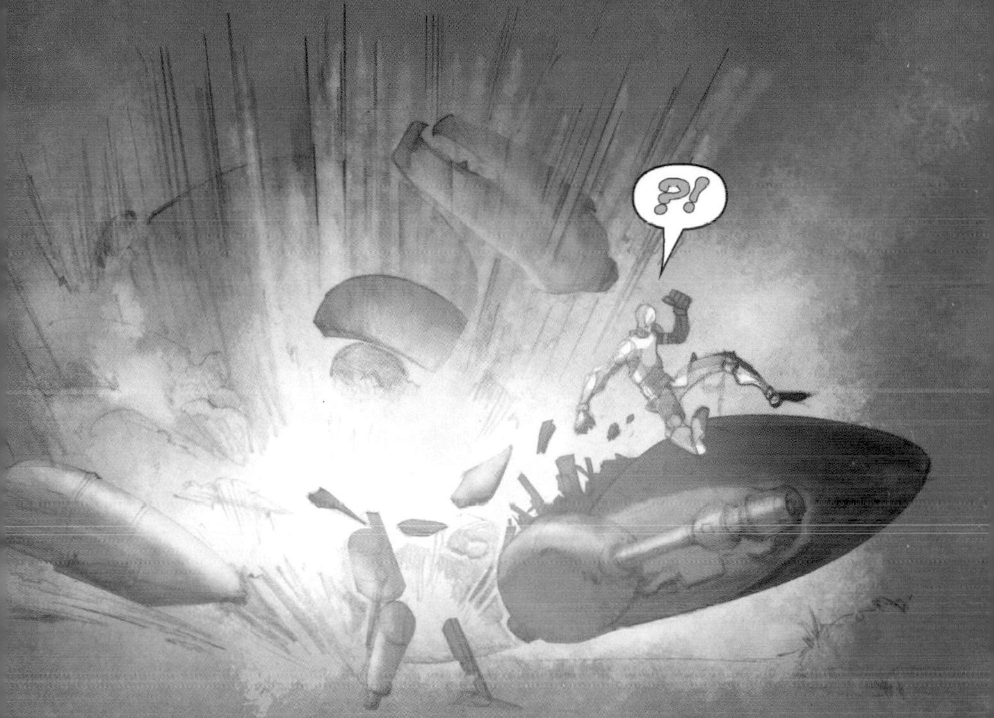
?!

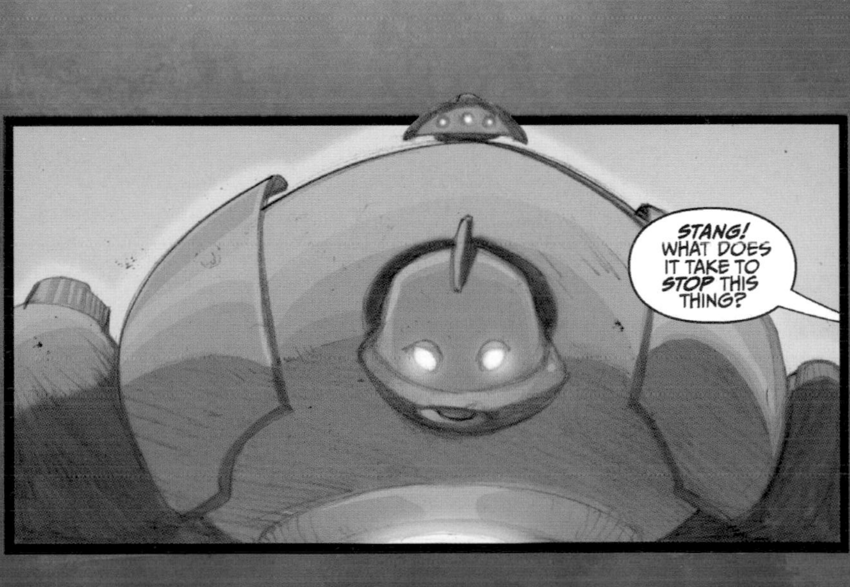
STANG! WHAT DOES IT TAKE TO STOP THIS THING?

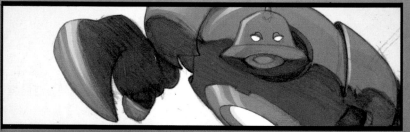

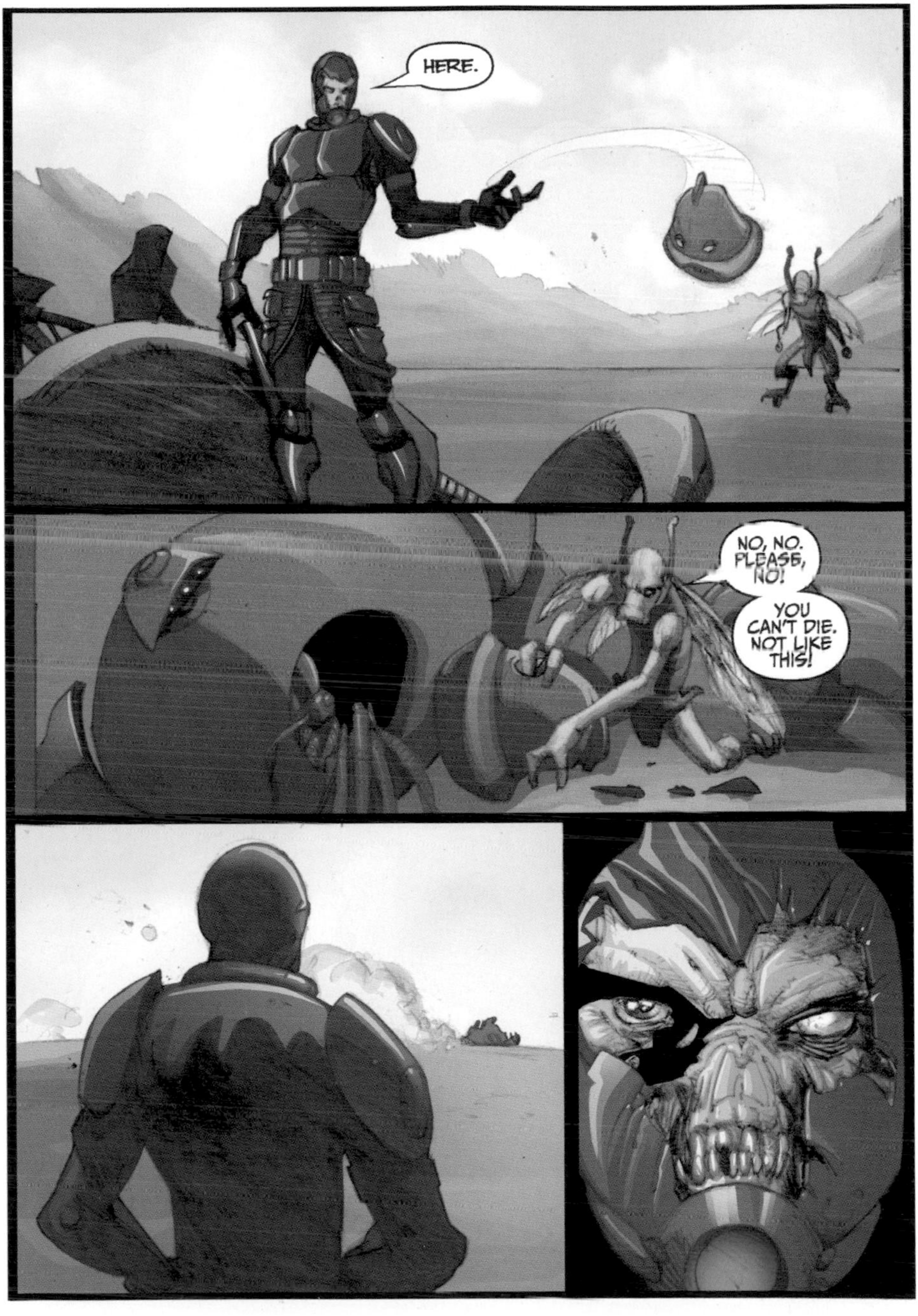

HERE.
NO, NO. PLEASE, NO!
YOU CAN'T DIE. NOT LIKE THIS!

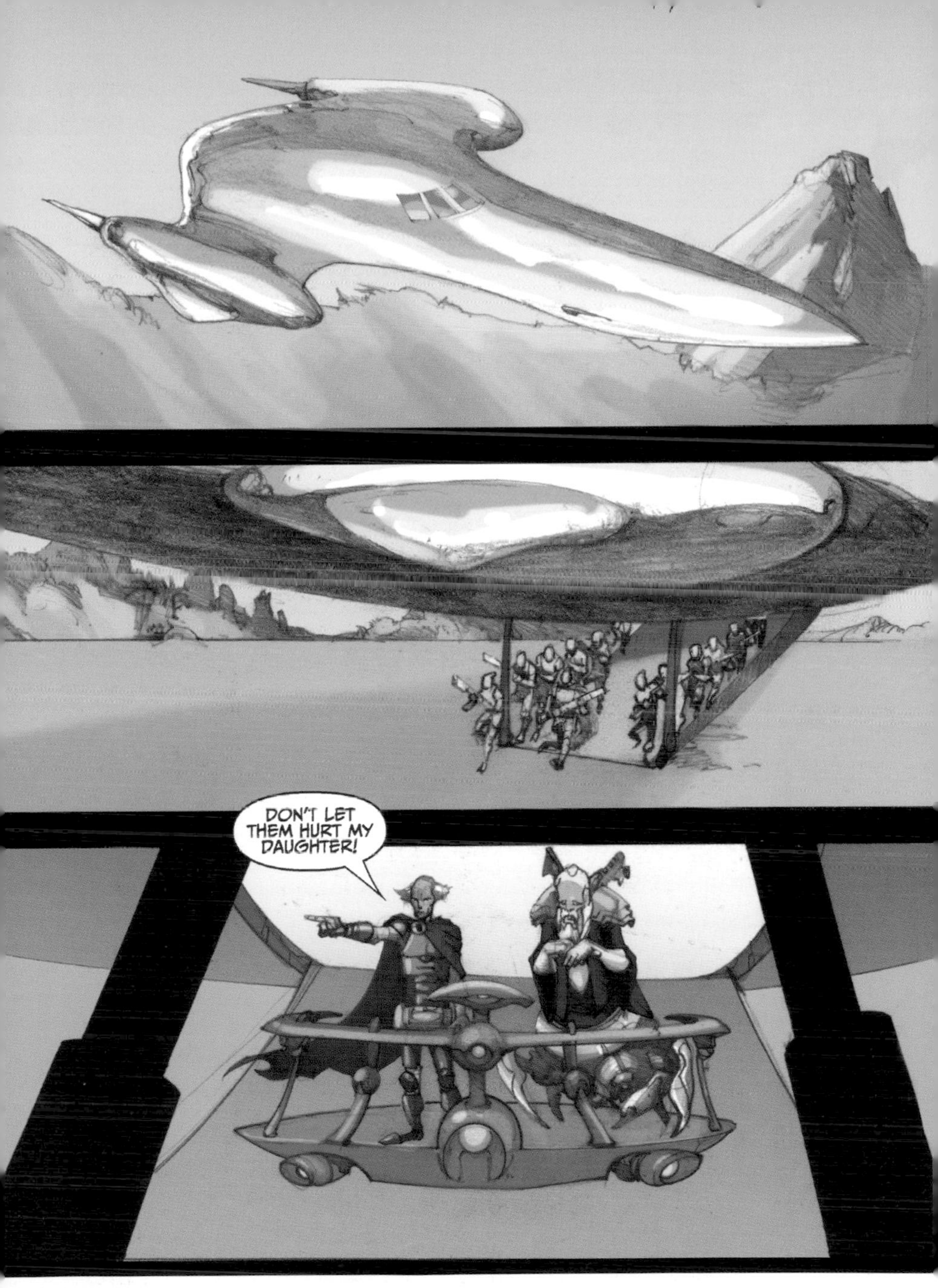
DON'T LET THEM HURT MY DAUGHTER!

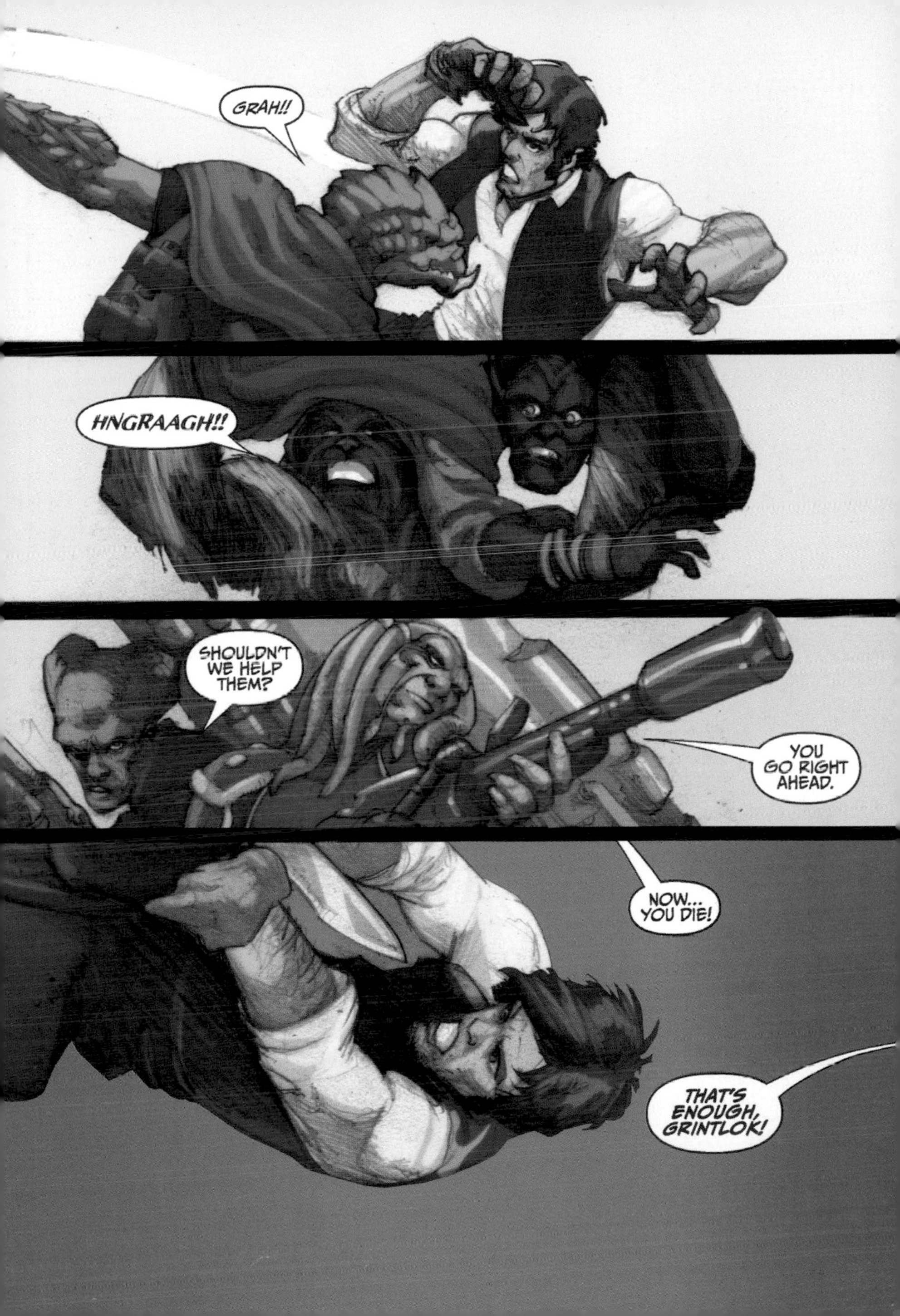
GRAH!!
HNGRAAGH!!
SHOULDN'T WE HELP THEM?
YOU GO RIGHT AHEAD.
NOW... YOU DIE!
THAT'S ENOUGH, GRINTLOK!

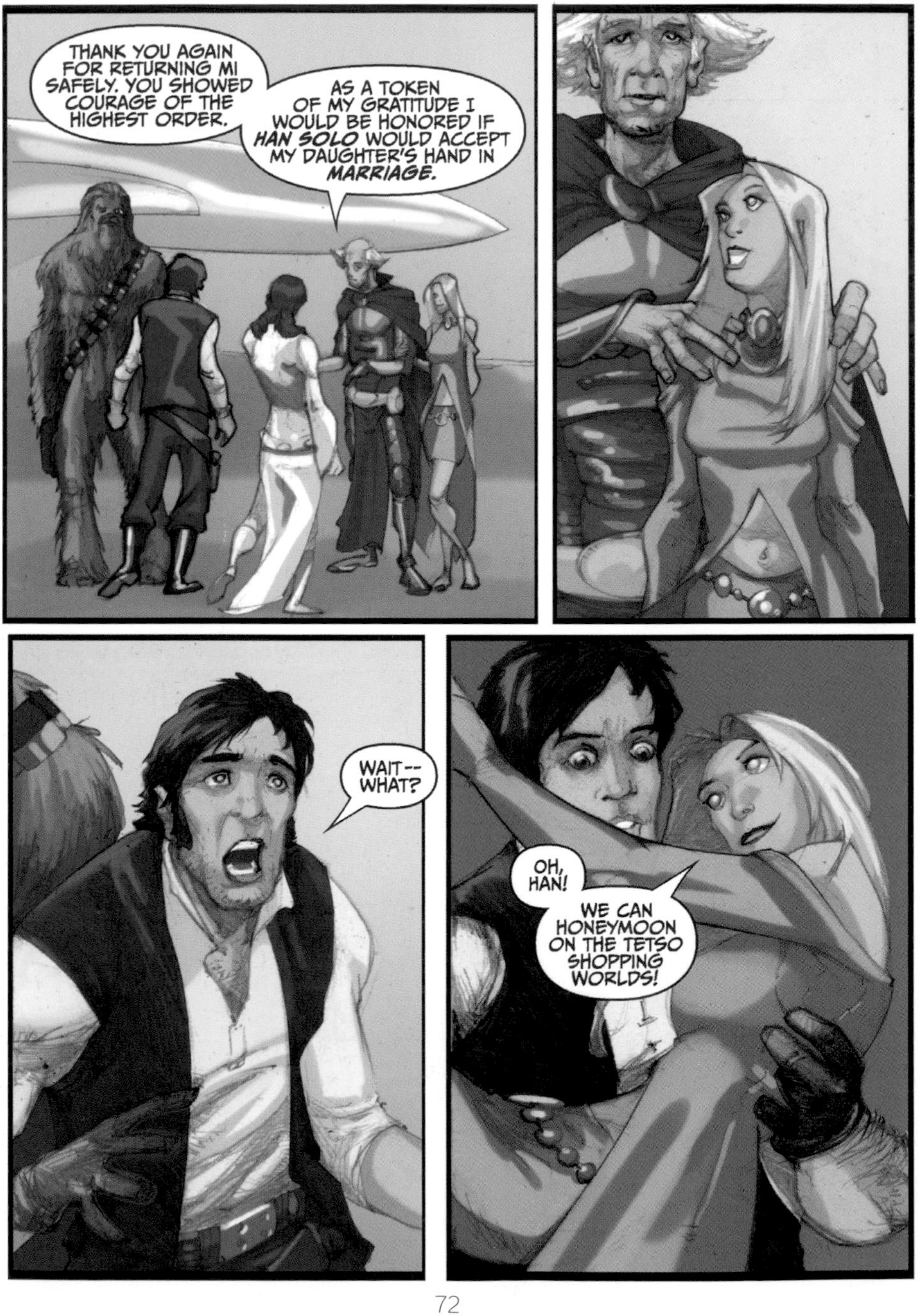
THANK YOU AGAIN FOR RETURNING MI SAFELY. YOU SHOWED COURAGE OF THE HIGHEST ORDER.
AS A TOKEN OF MY GRATITUDE I WOULD BE HONORED IF HAN SOLO WOULD ACCEPT MY DAUGHTER'S HAND IN MARRIAGE.
WAIT-- WHAT?
OH, HAN!
WE CAN HONEYMOON ON THE TETSO SHOPPING WORLDS!

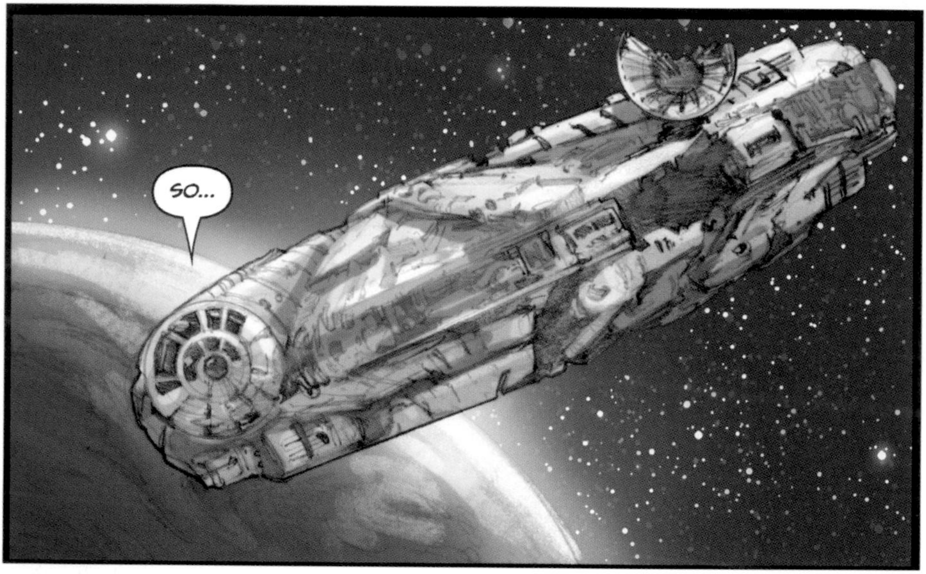
SO...

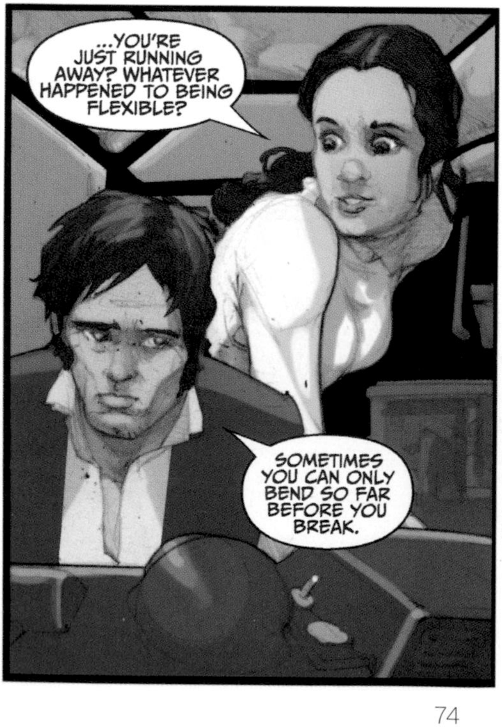
...YOU'RE JUST RUNNING AWAY? WHATEVER HAPPENED TO BEING FLEXIBLE?
SOMETIMES YOU CAN ONLY BEND SO FAR BEFORE YOU BREAK.

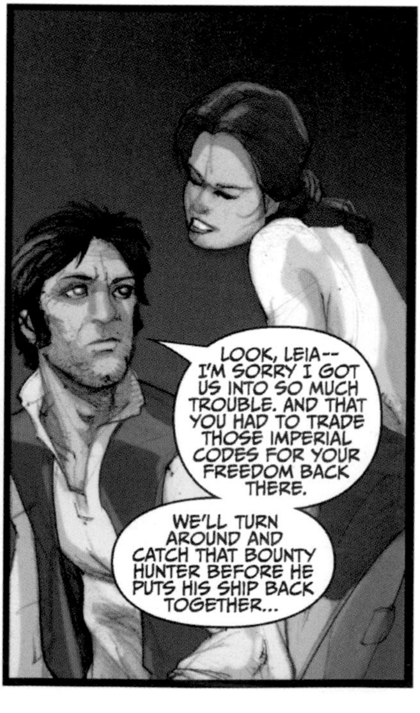
LOOK, LEIA-- I'M SORRY I GOT US INTO SO MUCH TROUBLE. AND THAT YOU HAD TO TRADE THOSE IMPERIAL CODES FOR YOUR FREEDOM BACK THERE.
WE'LL TURN AROUND AND CATCH THAT BOUNTY HUNTER BEFORE HE PUTS HIS SHIP BACK TOGETHER...

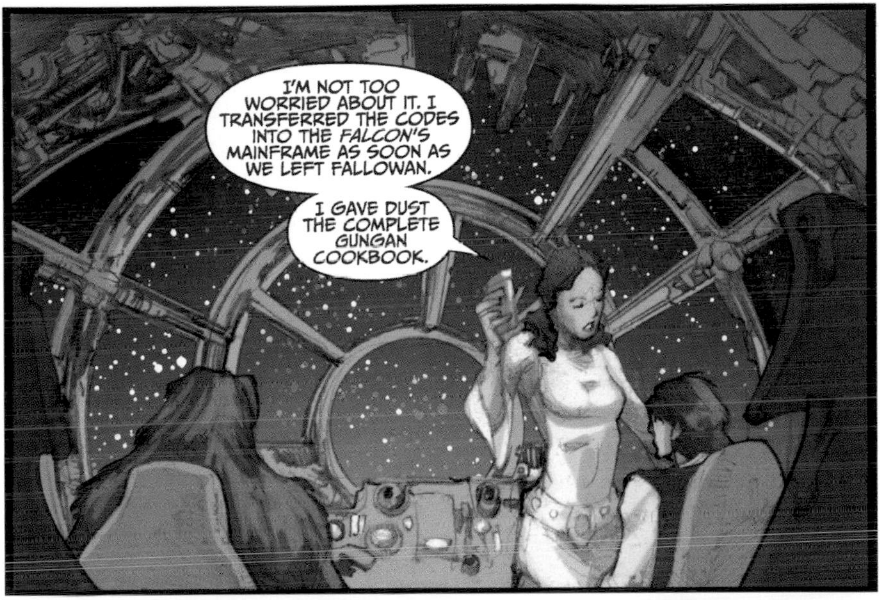
I'M NOT TOO WORRIED ABOUT IT. I TRANSFERRED THE CODES INTO THE *FALCON'S* MAINFRAME AS SOON AS WE LEFT FALLOWAN.
I GAVE DUST THE COMPLETE GUNGAN COOKBOOK.

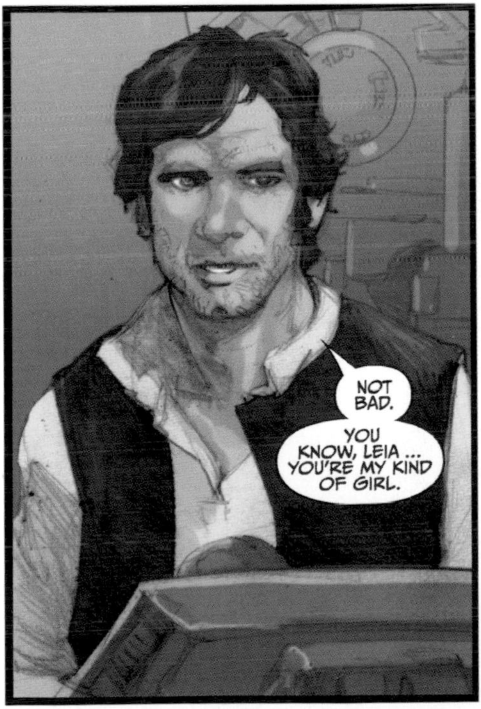
NOT BAD.
YOU KNOW, LEIA ... YOU'RE MY KIND OF GIRL.

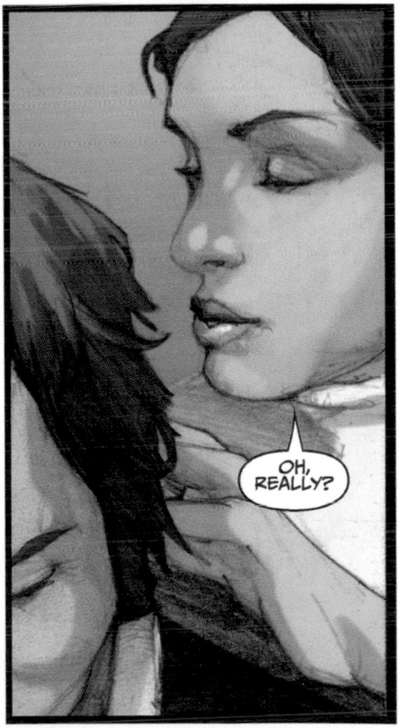
OH, REALLY?

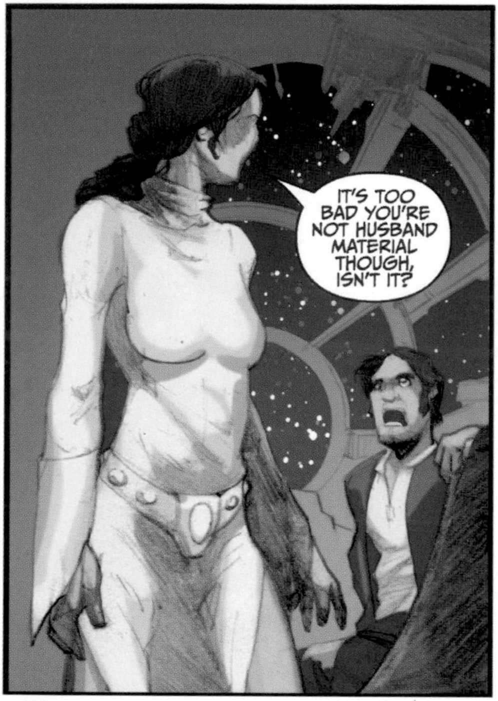
IT'S TOO BAD YOU'RE NOT HUSBAND MATERIAL THOUGH, ISN'T IT?

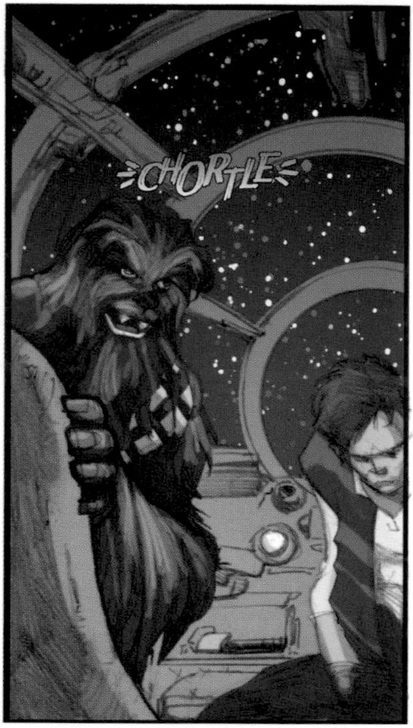
CHORTLE

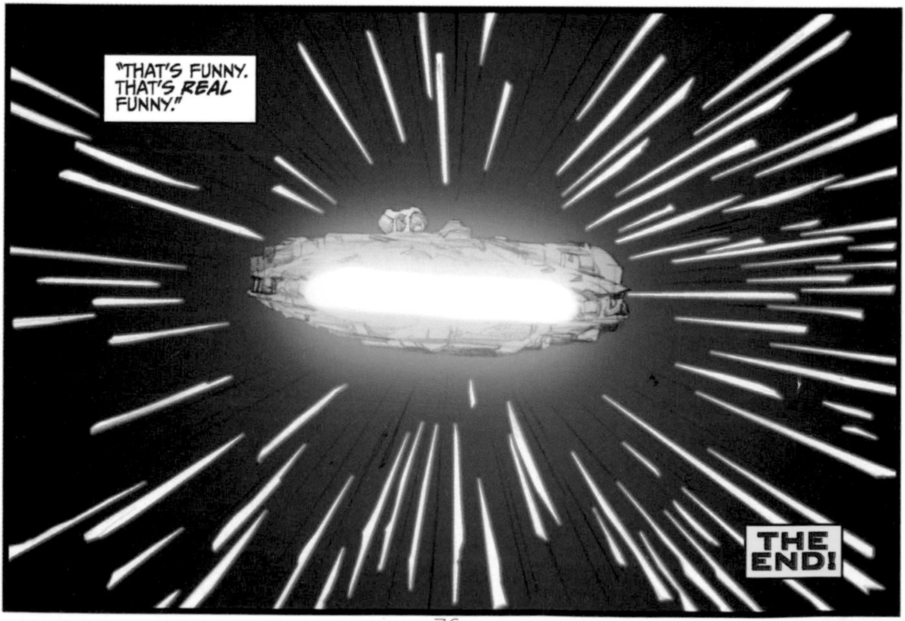
"THAT'S FUNNY. THAT'S *REAL* FUNNY."
THE END!